WHAT SEPARATES US

An Enemies-to-Lovers Romance

ANNE TROWBRIDGE

WHAT SEPARATES US

An Enemies-to-Lovers Romance

ANNE TROWBRIDGE

Cruz Into Love Series: Book 3

ISBN: 979-8-9865072-7-9

The chapter-opening graphics in this book are courtesy of Daisy Riley

For my sister, Amy.

*You're one of the smartest, strongest,
and funniest people I know.*

*Thank you for always being willing
to help me out, cheer me on, make me laugh,
and be one of my best friends
while you're at it.*

Other Books by Anne Trowbridge

Cruz Into Love Series

The Distance Between Us:
A Hidden-Identity Romance (Book 1)
(also available in Kindle Vella)

The Friendship Divide:
A Friends-to-Lovers Romance (Book 2)
(also available in Kindle Vella)

What Separates Us:
An Enemies-to-Lovers Romance (Book 3)
(also available in Kindle Vella)

The Curveball Incident Series

Curveball: A Love Story (Book 1)

Curveball: A Wedding Novella (Book 1.5)

Out of the Park: A Romance (Book 2)

Thrown: A Baseball Romance (Book 3)
(coming soon, but available now in Kindle Vella)

Sliding: Jim's Story (Book 4)
(coming soon, but available now in Kindle Vella)

Ticket to Love Series

The Honeymoon: A Second-Chance Romance (Book 1)
(also available in Kindle Vella)

The Bridesmaid: A Romantic Suspense Story (Book 2)
(also available in Kindle Vella)

Standalone Titles

Loving Out Loud: A Pop-Star Romance
(coming soon, but available now in Kindle Vella)

Chapter 1

Literally Annoying

"OH MITCH," she giggled, digging her perfectly polished nails into my thigh, "you're so funny!"

"No one's ever said that to me before in my life," I replied, tossing back another mouthful of beer as I assessed her. "I'm not exactly known as a comedian."

"Well, that's crazy because you literally are!" she went on, her hand now clutching my leg in a maniacally tight squeeze. "You make me laugh literally all the time!"

I rolled my eyes; I couldn't even help it. And yeah, I know it was a jerk thing to do. But I think it was her constant and incorrect use of the word "literal" that started poking holes in my attraction to her. *Pick a new word. Please, for the love of God, buy a thesaurus.*

Once I started noticing that, my brain then picked out every other little annoyance about her. Trust me, it was getting old. And as the stack of irritations grew, so did my unhappiness, both with her and with my whole life. I know it's stupidly inconsequential, and I do realize how ridiculous and baseless my building resentments were against Tifanee—yes, that's how she spells it. And yeah, okay, that's another of the many things I don't like about her. So sue me.

I get it—I really do. I understand that I'm not exactly coming off like a nice guy here. But then again, I guess I'm really *not* a nice guy. I used to be. And I think I'm still capable of it sometimes, too. I was nice to my baby brother and his new girlfriend, helping them out not long ago. So I'm not a total lost cause.

But what I am is weary. And angry. And lonely. I was tired of being all of those things, yet there I sat, with beautiful Tifanee and her stupid compliments driving a jackhammer through my last nerve.

"Mitchy, we've been together for six months now," she said as I silently tossed another item onto the stack. That "Mitchy" thing was just…what was I even doing with her? Every word out of her mouth created a dissonance in my head, and that had been true for a while. I don't know why she wasn't right for me. We'd met on a shoot—we're both models—and we'd produced enough chemistry together to make some really killer shots that day. I guess I thought that meant something. I noticed that chemistry, mixed it together with the attraction, and saw it as a possible lifeline. Something to hold onto when the rage builds inside me and the loneliness claws its way through my chest.

But I guess chemistry isn't the same as compatibility. And attraction sure isn't the same thing as love. She was beautiful; of course she was. And I think she's smarter than I give her credit for, because the more I started to pull back from her, the tighter she tried to hold on. Her holding on to me with both hands ended up displaying itself as a whole lot of fawning. She was constantly showering me with compliments, earned or not. That's why the "you're so funny" thing grated on me as badly as it did, rather than just wafting into the air between us—like any other harmless comment should—and floating away forgotten.

But I didn't want to just forget it and let it go. I was literally sick of her—yes, I know what I just did there—and I desperately needed to end the relationship. Because as lonely as I was, I didn't want *that*. I didn't want *her*. When you're with someone for months and still feel utterly alone, it's a pretty big hint that things aren't right.

"Mitchy?" she asked. "Did you hear me? We've been together for so long. I think it's time we moved in together. Why are we wasting money on two apartments? It's literally crazy when we could be together all the time."

"I heard you," I said curtly. Then came a vision of waking up and looking at her face across the top of my morning coffee every single day for the rest of my life, and it drove a shudder of repulsion through me. Yes, I actually, physically shuddered, and that definitely wasn't the reaction she was looking for, I'm sure. "Sorry, Tif, that's not what I want."

"But why drag out the inevitable?" she rambled on, not bothering to hide the hurt on her face. "What are we waiting for?"

"Honestly, I was waiting for this to feel right," I said, reaching down to peel her hand off my thigh. "But it doesn't feel right. And it never will."

"Are you…wait, are you *breaking up* with me?" Tears were forming in her eyes now. "No, I'm sorry! I didn't mean to push you. We don't have to move in together! Of course we don't. It was just an idea!"

"No, it isn't about that," I said, struggling to soften my words. "You didn't do anything wrong. You're a great person, and there's a man out there who will appreciate you. But that man can't be me."

"Why not?!" she said, the hurt turning to anger now. "Why can't it be you? We're great together!"

"I'm not happy," I said with a shrug. "I haven't been for a really, really long time. And I don't just mean with you. I'm not happy in any part of my life. Something happened recently that really drove that fact home for me. I'm not happy with me, so I don't have anything inside to offer to you."

"But whatever it is, we can get through it together!" she replied immediately. "You don't open up to me. That's the problem. You literally never talk to me. I didn't know something happened recently, but if you'd just share it with me, I can help you get through it."

"I appreciate that, I really do. But doesn't the fact that it never even occurred to me to talk to you about this tell you anything?"

She sat back, disbelief now mingled with the tears still shimmering in her eyes. "Why are you doing this? Why are you pulling away from me when you need me the most?"

"That's the thing, Tif. Even when we're together, I still feel alone. And I don't see that changing anytime soon."

She grabbed her purse with a haughty sniff. "That was a mean thing to say. I don't need this. I can have any man I want. And you're kind of a jerk, did you know that?"

"Sorry," I said, pulling some cash out of my wallet and throwing it on the table before standing up. "But you're right. I'm just not a very nice guy."

*   *   *

I figured ending things with her would help me somehow, or maybe it would lift a little of the darkness from my soul. But as I walked into my quiet apartment that night and crawled into bed, all I felt was the sting of that old, familiar loneliness—a loneliness that had somehow become my only companion.

"AND THEN I REALIZED he was literally going to pick a wide receiver in the first round," he said, stopping a moment to look at me. His eyes were wide with astonishment and expectation, like he was waiting for me to level up my reaction to match his. "Can you believe that?"

"Wow, that's crazy," I replied, hoping the response matched what he was expecting despite the uninterested tone. It must have, because he kept right on, immediately launching into a blathering description of the rest of his fantasy football draft. He employed the same energy and attention to detail that someone would use to analyze a breakthrough in the fight to cure all diseases.

"So, when it was my turn, I of course jumped on the best running back," he went on. "Like, duh, what was he even thinking? That position's just the safer move. Everyone knows that. It's where it's at when it comes down to it, you know what I mean?"

"No," I said, giving up even trying to follow the story. That was the thing with Sebastian that drove me crazy: He always talked *at* me, never with me. I don't think it ever once occurred to him that, since I don't watch football, maybe his position-by-position breakdowns of his imaginary team just weren't all that interesting or meaningful to me. Maybe if he tried to make football something we experienced together, it'd be different. But no, he had never once invited me to watch a game with him, where I'd presumably pick up a little knowledge about the sport. Maybe I'd even get why picking a running back in the first round was so awesome or whatever. But again, no. He just hung out with his buddies all the time and then spewed stats at me when we got together, like a high-powered lawn sprinkler. I was sick of being the grass.

"Are you even listening to me?" he asked, his eyes suddenly narrowing.

"Not really, no," I replied, not bothering to edit the words that came out of my mouth, as usual. I'll admit that's not my best trait, and I typically end up offending more people than I charm. There's just never been a filter inside me. As thoughts form, they fall out of my mouth without making any rest stops along the way in their journey toward sound. "I know you're talking about your fantasy football league, but since I don't even know the first thing about football, I kinda stopped listening a while ago. Running back, blah blah, draft, something something. Did I miss anything?"

"Tact," he said, his face crinkling into a look of disgust. "You missed tact. But then you always do, don't you?"

"Sorry," I said, wincing. Of course I knew it wasn't my best trait. I'd never be crowned Miss Congeniality, not that I'd be winning any beauty pageants anytime soon, either. I mean, I'm not ugly, but I'm definitely no stunner. Not like my best friend Lily, with her waterfall of golden-brown hair and her wide, blue, pixie-doll eyes. She's gorgeous, and she has a loving heart to match her beautiful exterior. Me, I'm more nondescript and forgettable; I'm harsh angles and jagged edges inside and out. My hair is neither blond nor brown.

Dirty blond, I guess people call it. My eyes aren't blue, and they aren't really green, either. Hazel isn't right. They're sort of a weird mix of all of that, and I never know which box to check when I'm renewing my driver's license. "Murky sludge" should be one of the choices.

"Yeah, that's the thing," Sebastian said, cutting through my self-reflection. "I don't think you are. Sorry, that is."

"Wait, I got lost again," I replied, my confusion genuine. "Are you mad because I didn't follow your rambling diatribe, or mad because I *told* you I didn't?"

"All of it, I guess. You know, honestly, this is just another example of why I'm getting tired of this. Tired of us. No, wait, I misspoke: I'm tired of *you*. I'm sick of the self-gratifying way you level everyone around you with your snarky comments. You have absolutely no regard for anyone's feelings. And then you toss out your little 'Gee I'm sorry about my honesty bombs, but that's just who I am' explanations, as though that makes everything alright. As though it excuses your behavior. I don't even know why I'm still with you. I don't even think I *like* you."

"Aww, come on, Seb," I said, trying to block out the pain his words were stirring up inside me. "Don't soften it. Tell me what you really think."

"Oh my God, I give up," he said, pulling out his wallet now and slamming bills down on the table. "You can't even help yourself, can you?"

"No, I guess I can't," I said, grabbing my purse and jacket. I'm always cold, even in a heatwave. Physically I mean, although I guess being emotionally cold is my thing, too. "Sorry I'm not who you want me to be. Good luck with your imaginary team and your imaginary future girlfriends who want to hear about it."

And that was the end of that.

*   *   *

We'd met after work, luckily, so I was able to stalk out of the sports pub and crawl into my junker of a car alone, along with my thoughts and the echoes of his flinty words.

I couldn't even be mad at him, really. He wasn't wrong, after all. And I wasn't particularly choked up or rattling around with achy pain at the thought of losing him. My emotions hadn't been too invested in the relationship for a while. Honestly, he'd done me a favor by initiating the inevitable.

But I *was* feeling pain of some kind. Feelings of remorse about my blatant character flaws were mixing together with memories of the words of a different man in my head. Like always, I'd said too much to that one, too, causing him to fling cutting words of his own at me, even in the middle of his family drama. I hadn't meant to make myself the focus of the conversation or inject any more pain into the middle of what was already a terrible and tense situation for him. But, well, this is me—and I hadn't been able to help myself.

Okay, I'm spitting out information with no context, like I accused Sebastian of doing. So here's the shortest explanation I can give: Lily's in love with Max, and Max has two brothers, Mitch and Jake. They're twins, and they're breathtaking; they're easily the most beautiful men I've ever seen. They recently staged a family video call to get a whole bunch of drama into the open so it could be aired out. It was the first time I'd ever seen or met Mitch, and I have to admit that something about him immediately reached through the screen and straight into my chest. He exuded this air of pent-up rage that's so startling because his brothers are both extremely selfless and sweet, almost to a fault. But not Mitch. No, he's this rolling, seething personification of energy and pain, and...I don't know. One look at him, and I was sucked right in.

And then...well, I immediately started saying whatever floated through my head—because of course I did—and I made him even more furious. Despite the crazy secrets that his brothers were using to carpet bomb everyone else, I somehow managed to make myself his focus and chief irritant.

This happened a few weeks ago, and I can still feel the bloom of embarrassment on my cheeks. I love Lily and Max so much, and I didn't mean to stomp around on everyone's feelings. Most of all, I certainly didn't mean to make the angry guy even angrier.

But I did, and now he's out there hating me, too, just like Sebastian. The weirdest part of all is that his disdain is still pushing me down into the dark waters of pain and self-recrimination.

Sebastian's, on the other hand, had barely caused a ripple.

Chapter 3

Family Dynamics

I WAS FEELING emotionally raw, and it had nothing to do with the breakup with Tifanee. Truth was, my emotions were *always* in a twist. They had been since my family melted down like a nuclear reactor back when I was a teenager. I'd been in exile from them for years, a recent family video call notwithstanding.

Jake had arranged the call to catch me up on all the latest news. As it turns out, my entire family was changing and evolving while I was sitting around building a list of reasons why Tifanee irritated me. Both my brothers were now in committed, loving relationships. Jake, my twin, had recently suffered a huge health scare, largely due to stress. That news was so painful I could barely let myself think about it. And our deadbeat father had killed a man with his car, which also resulted in him being comatose in a New Jersey hospital. That was a whole lot of stunning info to get hit with all at once. Any single part of it was lifechanging by itself, so the roll-up had been almost more than I could process. But I think the truth that hit me the hardest of all was that I quite clearly wasn't necessary or important in any of their lives. Not at all.

I mean, of course it wasn't shocking to me that time had marched on without me, after I packed my bags and bolted to California all those years ago. But knowing that and seeing its full effects were two different things. Our father was a drunk driver who killed a man. That man left behind a widow, who now was involved with Jake. She had a son, Liam, who I guess Jake now loved like his own son. And after all of those things happened, no one had even thought to loop me into any of it. If Lily hadn't shown up at my door one day looking for Max, I might not have known about his turnaround either.

Those feelings, and the realization that I was barely a blip on the radar of our family dynamics, made me lash out at them. I could have chosen to be hurt, or I could have been angry. I chose the latter, per usual. Then Jake swatted that anger right out of the air like the pesky fly it was. His response floated back into my mind again, leaving a path of destruction inside me that was as wide and painful as the first time I'd heard it—

Honestly, I got so used to handling everything alone that, in a way, it never even occurred to me to tell you. As with all of Max's struggles through the years, I was simply on my own. I didn't think you'd care or come help me shoulder it all. You never have before, right? So maybe I figured if I didn't tell you this time, you couldn't let me down again.

As his words clanged inside my head, I suddenly experienced a feeling of déjà vu. Where had I recently heard the phrase *It never even occurred to me to tell you?* Then the answer hit me like the ringing of a gong—*I* had said that barely even a day ago to Tifanee. Yeah, I'd told her that she was so inconsequential in my life that I never even considered opening up to her. But Jake had said that same thing to *me.* I was like the Tifanee in Jake's life. Irritating. An afterthought.

Then another, even more painful thought hit me—I didn't just feel lonely, I *was* alone.

I squeezed my eyes shut, trying desperately to push these pathetic feelings out of me. I'd made a choice a long time ago, after all, and I'd done it to protect the very family that had now moved on without me. I needed to focus on the good part of all of that, though, which was that it had *worked*. I'd succeeded in protecting them. Sure, it was looking like I might have destroyed myself in the process. But if I was presented with the same choice all over again, I'd choose my brothers every single time.

The other thing that I hadn't yet allowed myself to think about was how my dad's coma had the potential to change everything. With him out of the picture, maybe things could finally turn around for me. Maybe there was a chance I could even go back home...although whether or not I'd be welcomed was debatable.

As I let myself consider that possibility and try to envision what that might look like for me, my phone buzzed with an incoming text alert.

Max: I didn't want to do this, but I can't keep it bottled up inside me anymore, so I'm just going to come out and tell you that I'm furious with you.

Me: Hey little bro, great to hear from you, too.

Max: Not in the mood for jokes.

Me: Aw, c'mon, word on the street is that I'm quite a comedian.

Max: Just shut up a minute and let me rage at you. OMG you're so annoying.

I couldn't help chuckling here. Max hadn't talked for years thanks to trauma inflicted on him by our dad. Apparently, he'd bottled up a few words in all that time. I'd happily let him rage at me all day, though. This newly talking Max was a balm on my heart, mad or not.

Me: Sorry man. You caught me in a weird mood. What's up? Let me have it.

Max: I can't believe you took your anger and hurt out on Jake. Didn't you hear and understand what we were telling you about his health?

Me: Yeah, I heard it.

Max: There we were, telling you that he almost DIED, and it's been nothing but silence from you since you stormed off the call. He can't take any further stress right now. NONE. Only blood pressure medications and lowered stress are keeping him alive, and there you are, trying to make more reasons for him to worry.

Me: I'm sorry, man. You're right. I was actually sitting here trying to decide what to do about this very issue.

Max: Don't care what you do as long as you make Jake stop hurting over this. Actually, I take that back. I DO care what you do. Mitch, consider coming home. At least to visit. I know you probably don't feel this right now, but we miss you. And we need you.

I sat there for a moment, stunned by the power his words had over me. *Miss me? Need me? Really?* I couldn't imagine that was actually true. The evidence certainly said otherwise.

Me: I promise to think about everything you've said here. Thanks, Max.

I went to toss my phone aside, but on an impulse, I checked the price of flights to Newark first. I still wasn't sure what the best way forward might be, and I had a whole lot of thinking and soul-searching to do.

But it didn't hurt to at least compare a few prices.

Chapter 4

Girlfriend Time

I COULDN'T SEEM to shake the funk that Sebastian's words plunged me into, although I still didn't believe it had much to do with Sebastian himself. I mean, sure, I'd be lying if I said I didn't miss simply having someone around to be an automatic date or default set of plans. But I didn't really miss *him*.

Truthfully, his sudden departure from my life mostly cast a spotlight on how little time Lily and I had been spending together since she and Max became a thing. No Lily plus no Sebastian was equaling a whole lot of Just Claire. And me alone with my thoughts wasn't a healthy place to be lately. Not since that video call. Not since Ragey Ragerson had shot his slings and arrows at me. Normally that kind of sarcastic anger slides right off me. I couldn't figure out why this time had been different, especially since he really hadn't said all that much to me. I was starting to wonder if it was because that experience made me understand something—maybe I was starting to believe that my personality was so fundamentally flawed that I'd never be able to maintain a truly deep relationship. Not like the beautiful love that Max and Lily had found together. I mean, really, when a hot mess like Mitch Cruz thinks *you're* the hottest mess around, maybe it's time for some soul searching.

So, yeah, I was all up in my head and my feelings, and I missed my girlfriend time desperately. Lily was pretty much the only proof I had that I could form lasting human connections with someone outside my family. But I also had to face the fact that it was only because she's the personification of all that's good and kind in this world. Of course Lily loves me. She loves *everyone*.

With that thought, I picked up my phone and started texting—

Me: I miss you, Lils. I need girlfriend time. Stat.

Lily: Aww—miss you, too! Let's make plans. But is everything okay?

Me: …yes?

Lily: Gurrrrl. Talk to me.

Me: Aren't you busy with your man tonight?

Lily: I'm never too busy for you. And I'm trying to give him some space anyway. He's not really himself lately, not since everything went down with Jake. He just got done rage-texting Mitch.

The mere mention of Mitch sent my heart rate spiking. I wondered for a minute if I had a crush on Angry Jake-a-Like, but I dismissed that thought pretty quickly. I mean, c'mon, talk about banging your head against a wall. He was lightyears out of my league, he had hated me on sight, and he'd been a prickly manbaby to his sweet brothers. What was there to like about him? He wasn't just a red flag; he was a whole parade of red flags. You could fill a forest's worth of flagpoles like at the United Nations with all of his red flags.

Me: I'm sorry Max and Jake are going through all of that. And I'm sorry Mitch was such a d-bag about all of it.

Lily: Aww, no, he's not a bad guy. Really. They're all just hurting.

Like I said, Lily loves everyone. Naturally she could see the good in Mitch, despite the evidence to the contrary.

Lily: I think they all need each other. That's why Max asked Mitch to consider coming here, at least to visit. It would be so good for all of them, and maybe it would help heal the rift between them.

Me: Or maybe Mitch could just apologize and try being nice to them.

Lily: Lol. Well, yeah, that too. So you never answered my question. What's up with you?

Me: Nothing much. Well, except that Sebastian broke up with me because I don't understand running backs or something.

Lily: WHAT?!

Me: Kidding. He was blathering on about his stupid fantasy football league, and I got bored and told him that. He said he's sick of me and my lack of tact. So there you have it. Turns out I don't have any tact.

Lily: You? Um...where'd he get that idea?

Me: Very funny, Lils.

Lily: I'm sorry sweetie. You know I love you exactly the way you are. I adore that you tell me the truth no matter what. Everyone should have someone like you in their lives, and he just isn't smart enough to appreciate it. You're going to find a man—and trust me, he's out there just waiting for you—who will love how real and honest you are. He's going to find you refreshing and funny and amazing, just like I do.

Lily was the best human ever, and I sat there a minute, gripping my phone and fighting back a few threatening tears. I'm not a crier, like ever, so my reaction was more proof of just how off kilter I was feeling.

Me: Love you, Lily. You're the best friend in the world. Drinks after work tomorrow?

Lily: Sure! And hey, speaking of work, you made any decisions about that yet?

Me: Nah. Still just grinding cheese on already cheesed-up pasta dishes. Living the dream.

Lily: No thoughts yet on what you want to be when you grow up? Ballerina? Princess?

Me: Still thinking mermaid, but we'll see.

Lily: You'll figure it out. You're awesome like that.

Me: You are too. See you tomorrow!

I hit SEND, a smile on my face as I thought about Lily's words. As usual, talking with her had made me feel better. But it would take more than a blast of Lily's sunshine to fix all that was wrong. I was a twenty-five-year-old Olive Garden waitress with no clear vision of what I wanted to do. I also had a hubcap-less heap of a car, no boyfriend, and the personality of a rabid porcupine. What a catch I was!

For some reason, Mitch's beautiful face flashed in my head again, along with a startling thought—maybe I'd been drawn to him because we were the same. Maybe all that rage and d-baggery that I'd spotted in him was simply a reflection of my own.

Chapter 5

Therapy

PROBABLY WHAT I needed—probably what *every* person in my family needed—was therapy. Years and years of it, with teams of specialists from across the globe devoted to studying our boatloads of issues. But I'd been dealing with things on my own for a long, long time. One more set of bumps in the road wasn't likely going to change that anytime soon. Even though this particular set of bumps looked a whole lot more like mountain peaks.

But that didn't mean I couldn't see the value in releasing some of the ever-present anger inside me, which was right there like always, boiling under the surface like lava. Or...wait, is it called magma when it's still underground? I don't know. I'm a model, not a scientist—for lots of reasons, apparently. Anyway, my point is that I did actually have a way to release some of that pressure inside, and it involved a punching bag at the gym. I'd been going there for years, and that bag had absorbed a whole lot of anger and pain in a judgment-free setting. Win-win, although not necessarily for the bag.

I'd been going there so long, in fact, that I'd gotten kind of close to the owner. He was an old guy named Gus whose face was so craggy it looked like someone had carved him out of a rock. I'd formed very few true attachments in all my time in California, but Gus...well, he knew me as well as anyone. Probably isn't saying a lot, I guess, but I loved the old guy.

I was back there the day after Max's anger-fueled invitation to go home, wailing away on the bag with all the energy inside me. From the corner of my eye, I spotted a woman backing away, like the mere sight of me was terrifying. That made me feel even worse, which compounded the force I was throwing into those punches. Sweat trickling into my eyes was what finally stopped me. I peeled off the gloves, grabbed my towel, and mopped my face, pulling in a few deep lungfuls of oxygen as Gus ambled over for his daily check-in.

"Kid, when that thing finally rips or falls down, I'm mailing you the bill. So what's got you in such a state?"

"Same old garbage," I said, shrugging off his concern.

"Nah, I've seen you deal with your same old garbage before, remember," he said, his scratchy voice a *Why kids shouldn't start smoking* testimonial. "This ain't that, my boy."

I closed my eyes a minute, still intent on the task of mopping the sweat off my face, as I thought about his offer. Maybe it *would* actually help to get an outsider's viewpoint. Tifanee had made the same offer, but Gus's was tempting in a way hers hadn't been.

"Just a lot of family drama I'm trying to deal with, I guess," I said. "My twin brother, Jake, he…uh, well, he had a huge health scare. I could have lost him, which is terrifying but also kind of highlighting the fact that I'm not really a part of his life to begin with, you know?"

"Since this is the first time I'm hearing you got a twin, I'm gonna have to say that, yeah, Mitch, my boy, you're probably not that close with him."

I chuckled despite myself. "Communication just might not be my strong suit."

He nodded. "Yeah, you might want to stick with the modeling thing."

"My other brother told me I need to get my butt back home and make things right with Jake," I went on. "Guess I'm thinking about it. But that's a whole lot of change and drama and heartache, you know? Not sure I want to go backward."

"What do you have going on here that's so much more important than family?" he asked. "Do you have a single friend not named 'Gus, the Guy at the Gym'?"

"Well...no," I said, chuckling again. "I had a girlfriend, but I ended things with her the other day."

"Why do you think going home would be going backward anyway?" he asked.

"Whole lot of pain in my childhood," I replied, condensing way too much heartache into a very simple summary. "My dad was an abusive nightmare. He's in a coma right now, though. Doesn't look like he'll be coming back out of it, either."

The old man shrugged. "Mitchell, I don't know what you went through as a kid, or what's going on with your brothers. What I do know is that you about knocked my punching bag straight into next week with all that anger you got inside you. Something tells me you ain't never gonna be right until you deal with all that ugliness from the past. And nothing about that means you're moving backward. In truth, I'd say you'd finally be moving in the *right* direction. I think you've been doing nothing but standing still and marking time since you got to California."

*   *   *

Gus's words stayed with me for days. Was he right? Had I never formed attachments or laid down permanent roots in California because I'd simply been marking time and waiting until I could go home again? Waiting for things to change with the old man? Hoping he'd reconsider the terms of the deal we'd struck? Or had I simply been biding my time until he died?

Maybe all of those questions could be answered with a resounding *yes*. And if all of it was true, then something else was true too—my dad's coma might have released me from this paralysis I'd been living in.

So yeah, maybe it really *was* time to go home.

Chapter 6

Regressing and Regretting

SO MANY OF my fellow servers were either late or called in sick the next day that I ended up staying way past the scheduled end of my shift. I had to cover while the managers frantically tried to pull in more people. And by the time I left the restaurant, Lily was home and tucked onto her couch for the night.

Me: Sorry our girlfriend time got messed up! Tomorrow?

Lily: Ugh, no, tomorrow's bad. I'm sorry tonight's not working out either. I feel like such an old lady, but I'm just too tired to move off this couch.

Me: You do have a nice yet tiny couch.

Lily: I'm at Max's, but his is comfy too!

Me: Oh yeah duh.

Of course she was at Max's.

Lily: We'll find time to get together soon! But not tomorrow. Max and I are having dinner with Melody, Jake, and Liam. I'll let you know what does work though, once Max and I talk about our upcoming plans. I'm just not sure what's up.

Me: Sure, no worries!

Okay, that was a lie because I had lots of worries. Many, many worries. All the worries. It was getting harder and harder to find time to hang out with Lily since she and Max got together, something I totally understood, of course. But Max was her priority now. His family was her family. I'm not gonna start hiding the truth, either, so I'll just blurt this out, Claire-style: I didn't want to get edged out, but sometimes I felt like I was.

That reminded me of Mitch's words on the phone call, when he accused his brothers of pushing him out of their circle of trust. I could sympathize. And, yes, that was just more proof that he was always sitting there at the top of my thoughts, for reasons I still didn't really understand.

Going back to my apartment sounded lonely and depressing, so I decided on an impulse to drop in at my mom's house. Mom time is still girlfriend time, sort of. When I pulled up, I was surprised to see my brother's Jeep out front. I parked behind him and clattered inside loudly so I wouldn't startle her. She's the jumpiest human on the planet.

"Hey, Mom!" I said, plopping onto the couch next to her and leaning over to pop a little kiss on her cheek. Then I threw in, "Chad, haven't seen your ugly face in a while."

"We look alike, you idiot," he replied cleverly. You wouldn't know it, but mostly we're pretty close, potshots notwithstanding.

"What brings you by, sweetie?" my mom asked. Only my mom and Lily think I'm anything approaching "sweet."

"She's probably here to whine because tonight's another round of the draft for Sebastian's team," Chad observed, not even looking at us as he messed around with something on his phone.

"How would you even know that?" I asked. "And we broke up anyway."

"I'm in the same league with him," Chad replied. "And, hah! I knew it would happen eventually.

Although word on the street is that *he* dumped *you*."

He topped that last comment off with a maniacal laugh, so I leaned over and punched him in his stupid arm, knocking his phone to the floor. I mimicked his laugh right back at him, causing my mom to jump with a startled, "Oh my!" That sent Chad and me into hysterics since she never disappoints with her startled reactions. My poor mother. Chad and I regress about twenty years when we get together, but I swear we're basically cool with each other. Mostly.

"Oh, honey, I'm sorry about Sebastian," she said, wisely choosing to ignore our antics. "He was always so polite."

"Mmm-hmm, yeah. I got sick of him talking at me about all his stupid football crap, and he got sick of me being blunt about things like how boring his stupid football crap is. Let's call it mutual."

"Bozo," Chad inserted helpfully.

"I was supposed to go out with Lily tonight," I continued, ignoring him, "but I got stuck at work. So I decided just to swing by here and say hi."

"Aww, I'm glad you did," Mom said. "How's Lily doing?"

"She's the happiest she's ever been. She met this amazing guy, and they are ridiculously, awesomely in love. If I didn't love her so much too, I'd hate her for it. They are next-level grossly cute together."

"Thought she was in love with me," Chad said. "Whatever happened to the days of her following me around with those big cartoon eyeballs of hers fluttering at me?"

"I told her what a jerk you are, and I told her what you said about her. Trust me, she couldn't forget about you fast enough."

"You did *what?!*" he said, putting down his phone, his tone losing the taunting edge and turning serious. "What exactly did you tell her?"

"It was after I suggested you take her to that work function, and you were such a creep about it, remember? You said all that horrible stuff about how being with her would be like…I don't know, something like pixies riding unicorns or whatever. You really hurt her feelings."

"No, *you* really hurt her feelings!" he fired back, the anger in his eyes no longer playful. "Obviously I wouldn't have ever said that stuff to her *face*. I wasn't attracted to her, but I've always liked her as a person. I thought I could trust you not to annihilate your supposed best friend and break my confidence this way. Being mean to Lily is like kicking puppies. Oh my God, Claire. Seriously, what is *wrong* with you?"

"I didn't want her holding onto some stupid fantasy life with you that was never going to happen!" I pretty much yelled. "Of course my goal wasn't to hurt her—it was to set her *free!* And guess what? I was right! She met Max almost immediately after that conversation, and he's quite clearly the love of her life. I did her a favor!"

"Just because it accidentally worked out for her doesn't mean you did the right thing," he carried on, picking up his phone and rolling his eyes. "I have a lot of sympathy for Sebastian right now."

"Then maybe *you* can date him."

"Honey, I think Chad has a point," my mom said. "You probably didn't go about that the right way. You needlessly hurt Lily, and you embarrassed your brother."

"See?" Chad said. "Even Mom's on Team Sebastian."

I sighed and tried to battle back the choking feeling of regret that seemed to be crawling up my throat.

Girl time at Mom's was not a ton of fun, it turns out.

Chapter 7

Options and Anger

GOING HOME? Would it really be possible?

Once I allowed that thought to get even the tiniest foothold in my mind, it started stalking me like a predator every single moment, despite a sudden uptick in bookings. I had another gig at a local Harley dealer, for example. My long hair and tattoos screamed "motorcycle rider" apparently, despite the fairly unremarkable SUV I drove. And I shot a cover for a romance book too. Thankfully, Tifanee wasn't the other model. Regrets and memories were slithering around in my skull nonstop, but breaking up with her sure wasn't part of that. Although I guess I did regret not doing it sooner. And I regretted hurting her. See? I'm not a complete monster.

But throughout all of that, my mind was holding up that thought in a bright spotlight—that idea of going home after all these years—and analyzing every angle and side of it. Partly, I was thinking about simple logistics, like would I lose a lot of work? The motorcycle dealer probably wouldn't be paying to fly me out for future shoots, but many of my jobs weren't local anyway. Likely a shift to the East Coast wouldn't affect my career all that much. It might even grow if I could talk Jake into coming with me for jobs that might require twins. We'd done it before and, believe it or not, there was a lot of opportunity there. Jake had stuck mostly to the personal training gig, however, and kept the modeling to a side-hustle. I was the opposite and had focused primarily on modeling, although I'd completed the necessary steps to be a trainer, too. Eventually the modeling would dry up, and I wanted options.

After I'd thoroughly dissected every part of the idea, I decided my biggest issue was my lease, which I'd recently re-signed. That would be a problem.

Actually, that wasn't even the full truth. The biggest issue of all had nothing to do with practical things like jobs, apartments, and money. The really big issue had to do with my dad. My brothers had painted a bleak picture of his health. Long story short, he likely wouldn't be recovering.

But what if he did...?

Boom! That was the problem. My dad and I had come to an agreement a long time ago. I'd held up my end of the bargain by leaving and staying gone, taking what I knew with me. And he'd done his part by dialing back the abuse of Max and allowing Jake to take over as Max's father, essentially. But if I moved back and then the old man woke up? His revenge would be swift, and all the secrets I'd worked so hard to protect Max from might come flowing right out of his giant, ignorant mouth. Maybe he wouldn't care if everyone knew. Or he might jump right back into his old patterns of abuse.

And then what would happen?

Would Max regress? Would he break things off with Lily and climb right back into his self-imposed prison? Or was he strong enough to resist now? Was I killing myself to protect him from something that he'd now be able to manage, and from shock he could eventually absorb? Seriously, though, who even knows, because maybe he'd be just fine with it instantly. Maybe I'd done all this for nothing.

I didn't know the answers to any of these questions, and I sure didn't want to play a dangerous game of chance with Max's life. I couldn't make a snap decision that had possible debilitating ramifications for my brother.

Okay, so maybe that's why I couldn't permanently move back, at least until the old man actually died. But none of that would stop me from simply visiting, right? If our father woke up from his coma while I was there, I could vanish again with no harm done. My newly signed lease wouldn't really allow an easy change of coasts anyway, so I wasn't even sure why a feeling of anger that felt fueled by disappointment was igniting inside me.

It didn't matter, though. Angry and disappointed or not, it was going to have to be good enough. I'd book an open-ended ticket and check out the situation for myself. *There*, I thought, *problem solved*. And, honestly, who knows? Maybe Max was overselling how upset Jake was. Maybe our dad would soon spiral right down the drain, ending his pathetic existence. And maybe all those long-buried secrets would stay safely entombed right along with him.

Yeah, okay, it was a decent plan and compromise. It answered a lot of questions and allowed for a certain level of flexibility. Really, now that I'd come to that decision, my remaining issue was that I'd have to find a way to live cheaply in New Jersey so I could keep up with the monthly payments on my apartment.

I didn't even know what my brothers' living situations were, I suddenly realized. Did they have guest space for me? As soon as I considered that, I dismissed it. They were both knee-deep in the honeymoon stages of new relationships. I didn't want to third wheel on top of either of those situations.

That only left one other cheap solution...but as soon as the thought of staying in my childhood home with my mom floated through my head, I could feel anger ballooning up inside of me and filling any available spaces it could find. *How am I not the one on blood pressure medication?* I thought dully as I tried to tamp those feelings back down. My automatic response quickly answered at least one question—there was no way I'd ever step foot back inside that house. The whole reason I was even out here in the first place was all their fault, both my mom's and my dad's. Their actions and inactions and failures as parents—and even as human beings—were what I had been forced to pay the price for all those years ago. Jake and Max had also suffered, of course, and they'd suffered more. But at least they'd had each other. Thanks to my parents, I'd had no one.

Selfishly, I was also mad that no one even knew that I'd paid a price, too. That's why Jake had accused me of abandoning him and leaving him to deal with everything alone. He didn't know the whole truth, so I ended up looking like the bad guy. I was the deadbeat loser who couldn't handle the heat of the fire that consumed our family. My brothers stayed to battle it; they thought I ran away like a coward.

I know, I know—I fled with all of those secrets scorching their deadly path through me, so of course my brothers weren't aware that I didn't abandon them. Not really, anyway. They didn't know because I'd made sure they never would.

So I guess some of my festering anger was aimed at myself. Maybe I shouldn't have left. There were lots of reasons to believe that, in my teenage fears and panic, I'd made the wrong decision. Maybe it would have been better for Max to deal with it back then, but now we'd never know. I was angry that I'd been forced to choose, and I was even more furious because I might have gotten it wrong.

In the end, what it came down to was that I hated my parents for what they'd done. But I hated me, too. And that's the heart of the reason why I had nothing to offer Tifanee, or anyone else for that matter.

There wasn't anything inside me worth giving.

Chapter 8

Salt and Bad News

WHEN LILY GETS depressed, she starts packing cookie dough into her cheeks like a squirrel. I'm not much different, although my secret shame is chips—tortilla, potato, cheese-dust-infused puffs, doesn't matter. I'm sure there's a "that's because I'm always so salty" joke hanging out there on the tree, low and easy to pick. But I wasn't feeling like joking that evening, not when I could abandon attempts at humor and walk away on a journey to see what other salty goodness I could find.

It had been a while since that whole disaster at my mom's house, and I still hadn't been able to shake the regret. Of course, I couldn't seem to lose the loneliness that had been chasing me around the dance floor of my pity party, either. It had been one thing after another with Lily lately, and we still hadn't managed to find any time to spend together. I mean, I really shouldn't have been upset about it because the reasons were varied and valid, and some of them had nothing to do with her. I'd been getting scheduled for more evening shifts lately, so our schedules weren't lining up. But it wasn't just that. Max was upset about everything to do with his brothers, including the fact that no one had heard from the apparently also-still-salty Mitch. And this was despite Max's angry attempts to get him to show his face in Jersey. So Lily was focusing all her free time and energy toward her man and the lifting of his spirits.

I got it and understood, of course. But it still sucked, especially since I'd been kind of lying low and hiding from my own family. I was still licking my wounds after my mom and Chad both tore into me about how I handled ending Lily's crush on him. Deserved or not, their comments had stung.

So there I sat, with only my bags of chips to keep me company, when someone rang the doorbell. No one ever just shows up unannounced at my door, and I mean no one. When my family or Lily come over, they text to tell me they're on their way. If packages arrive, the drivers shotput them onto the stairs out front and declare it good enough. So to say I was shocked was an understatement. Not even sure I knew I had a doorbell, to be honest.

When the bell rang, I did a jumpy cringe comparable to anything my mom had ever produced. Then I set the chip bags aside, brushed off the salt and crumbs, and headed to the door. I cautiously opened it to find my sweet landlady standing there. I rented out what's probably technically an in-law suite in her house. It's a pretty cozy arrangement, too—I've got my own outside entrance, she's endlessly quiet, and she lets me park my Corolla in her driveway. The truly amazing part is that the rent isn't very high, and the utilities are included. She keeps the heat cranked up year-round, it feels like, because she's always cold. But since I am, too, we're like the perfect housemates.

"Hi, Mrs. Anderson," I said, a little embarrassed about the chip buffet still laid out on the couch and hoping she wouldn't want to come inside. "Is everything okay? I'm not late with the rent, am I?"

"No, dear, but would you mind if I came in?" she said, darn it. "I need to talk to you."

Ooh, maybe she's here to tell me what a bad friend I am, too, I thought as I opened the door and shot one more red-faced glance over at my cringey junk food. Oh well. *If she doesn't want to walk inside my depression, maybe she could just call next time,* I thought as I gestured for her to come inside.

"I'm sure you're wondering how long it took me to whip up this fancy meal," I said, grabbing the bags off the couch and moving them to a side table. Yeah, that was way better.

"You're fine, dear," she assured me, settling down on the couch as I joined her. I couldn't exactly begrudge her plopping down there, interrupted pity party or not. It was her couch, after all. That was the other thing that made the apartment a steal: It came furnished.

"Claire," she said, taking a deep breath that ratcheted up my nerves. I had a feeling I wasn't going to like whatever she was about to say. "You know I have a son, right?"

"Sure," I said. "Uh…I want to say…Jim?"

"Lawrence, dear," she said. "He and his wife just had a baby, and they need some help right now. The thing that would work the best for all of us would be if they could move in here, with me."

"Huh," I said. "Are you warning me that a baby's going to be crying all night and keeping us up?"

"Not quite," she said. "There's just no room for all four of us in my part of the house, not with all the things that newborns need. The best situation for everyone would be if they took that side of the house, and I moved to this side."

"Are you asking to be my roomie?" I joked, even though I was pretty sure I knew what she was really saying. "We could tell secrets and curl each other's hair."

"No dear," she said with an embarrassed wince. "Although that sounds lovely, I'm hoping you wouldn't mind terribly moving out. As soon as possible. You and I never had a formal lease, and I realize that you could fight me on this and probably win. But, well, I was just hoping that a sweet girl like you would do the kind thing and let this happen. For me. And for Lawrence and my grandbaby."

Part of me wanted to tell her that her lazy leech of a son should maybe have made sure he could afford a home for his baby before actually having one. But for once I lassoed my words before they galloped out of my mouth. She'd been nothing but kind to me for years. The least I could do is vanish out of her life on command.

"Sure, Mrs. Anderson," I said. "Is two weeks okay?"

"Oh, well, yes, that would be…sure," she said. The way she stumbled over her words made it clear that she was hoping it'd be sooner.

"But hopefully I can get out of here even quicker than that," I added. The smile that met my comment confirmed my suspicions: She wanted me gone, like, yesterday.

I made a few minutes of what I hoped was benignly pleasant conversation, but the whole time I was eyeing those chips. I couldn't wait for her to leave.

I had a whole new set of feelings to eat.

Chapter 9

Stuck

ONCE I MADE the decision to go home, I thought everything would fall into place pretty easily. I figured I'd book a flight, pack a bag, then let my brothers help me figure out a cheap landing spot.

But it wasn't unfolding like that. I couldn't seem to gather myself together enough to pull the trigger on booking the flight or packing the bag. I was mentally and emotionally stuck, and I think that was because I couldn't quite bring myself to face Jake. He'd accused me of abandoning him, and I know that's exactly what it must look like from his point of view. I was afraid I'd blurt out stuff I had no business saying in an attempt to justify my actions. If I didn't talk to him, I couldn't trip over a pile of trauma-dumping, basically.

But I suppose that wasn't the whole truth either. I mean, it *was* that, but it was more than that, too. Jake and I were twins; we were two sides of the same coin. Finding out that he'd almost died was doing something to my soul, and it was something I didn't like and sure didn't want to face. Losing him would have meant losing *me,* and that's just the way it was.

Even though we were essentially estranged, and even though we hadn't seen each other in person all that much in years, we were bound together. If he had died in his truck instead of putting it in park and merely passing out, we both would have died in some ways. Feeling that sensation, the one that said we'd brushed past tragedy and somehow emerged mostly unscathed...I don't know. It should have been making me feel nothing but gratitude. But, like almost everything else in my life, all it was doing was throwing gasoline on the fire burning inside me. The truth of the matter is that I should have been there for him. I should have been there all along. But I hadn't been, and he would have died feeling the sting of my absence. It was a pain that wasn't ever going to heal, and I was sick of feeling that way. But I couldn't imagine ever finding a way to extinguish it or soothe my soul.

I toyed with contacting Max instead, but I knew he was also bitterly disappointed in me. Jake was the golden hero who'd jumped in to save him, scooping him right out of trauma and lovingly nudging him into a beautiful future. I was the deadbeat who'd had no qualms walking away and never looking back for years. Facing him and knowing how he surely must feel about me hurt, but I'd never been forced to own up to it before. Jake and I had met up on some of those photoshoots I mentioned, the ones that needed twins, so I'd seen him and interacted with him a bit over the years. But no one—aside from Jake—had interacted with Max. My limited relationship with him had always been via text. Hearing him talking on the video call was a happy shock since I hadn't heard his voice since he was a kid. Not exactly a warm and loving bedtime story I'm telling here, but that's just the way things were— and the way they'd unfortunately needed to be.

It all left me feeling broken, raw, and unsure, so I tried to shelve it all for a little longer and turn my focus to the practical stuff first. I decided it was time to run my plans past my agent, Janet. She wasn't exactly a warm and fuzzy person, but she'd been ferocious about helping me grow my career. Even when I was inexperienced and just starting out in the business, she'd always made me feel like I was in good hands.

"Hey, Mitch," she said when she answered my call. "Nothing new to report. Although I meant to tell you those shots you did for that cover the other day were electric. Client was raving."

"Oh, good, that's great to hear," I replied, the lie falling easily out of my mouth. My mind was tied in too tight of a knot to care much. "Do you think you could keep the work flowing if I relocated to the East Coast for a while? You see any potential problems?"

"No, not really. There's this new technology they're experimenting with called 'airplanes,' so that might just be the break we need to pull it off."

"Funny. Okay, good. Because I'm not sure how long I'll be staying."

"Why, what's up? You okay?"

"Family stuff," I told her, fairly confident she wouldn't push for more. I was as close to Janet as I was to almost anyone in my life. Which, of course, meant she knew almost nothing about me.

"Mitch, if it wasn't for your brother occasionally agreeing to do jobs with you, I wouldn't even know you *had* a family."

"Yeah, there's Jake, of course. And we've got a younger brother, Max."

"He as hot as you and Jake?"

I chuckled. "Stop trying to drum up more clients, Janet. Modeling definitely wouldn't be his thing— although, yeah, he's a good-looking kid."

"Good genes. I like it."

"Oh yeah, we're swimming around in quite the amazing gene pool," I said. The very thought of who was responsible for those genes, and their award-winning parenting skills, had me rolling my eyes. "Okay, well, I'll keep you posted, but this is happening soon."

"No problem. Good luck."

"Thanks."

*　　　*　　　*

I still needed to do things like forward my mail and talk to my landlord. But all in all, I was running out of minutiae to focus on instead of what I really needed to do. So, with a deep breath and long exhale, I opened a text and entered both my brothers' names.

There was no more avoiding it. It was time to let them know I was heading home.

Chapter 10

Lily's Perfect Solution

I SLIPPED INTO some sort of fugue state after my sweet little landlady threw me under the bus that was driven by her son's poor life-planning skills. I knew what the simplest solution was, though. I just needed to pack up my suitcases, a few boxes of books, and whatever junk I'd accumulated. Then I'd do the dreaded Walk of Shame back home to my mom's house. That was the fastest answer to the problem, as it would get me out of Mrs. Anderson's life within twenty-four hours. Since I didn't have that much stuff—like I said, the apartment came furnished, even down to the pots, pans, and dishes—I wouldn't need a team of professional movers. No, just me, my Corolla, and my depression. The three of us were up to the task, I was sure of it.

But I was dreading it, and I wasted a few days avoiding any steps toward actually executing those plans. Like calling my mom, for example. Or pulling out the suitcases. Those kinds of steps.

My guilt was eating away at me, though, and I knew Mrs. Anderson was dying to have me out of there. So, during one particularly awful shift wherein a lady ripped into me about how overcooked her steak was—girl please, you're eating steak at a pasta joint— and then I managed to drop a tray with two big salads on it, sending lettuce flying through the air like confetti, I decided I may as well just call my mom and keep the ball rolling. Who was I trying to kid, anyway? It wasn't like my current life was such a golden set of crowning achievements. What was one more embarrassing setback?

I got home, flopped on the couch, and kicked off my shoes, then pulled up my mom's name in my list of contacts. Right as I was about to call her, though, a text arrived. And yes—of course I happily let it distract me.

Lily: Okay, I know I said today wouldn't work, but if I don't see my Claire I'm going to explode. Can I come over?

Me: Yes x infinity.

Lily: On my way.

I eyed my mom's number a while longer, then I decided I'd call her later.

I needed to go shower and throw on some leggings and a t-shirt anyway.

*   *   *

When Lily got there, she squealed and swept me into a hug that employed a vacuum-like force. I ate the whole thing up and hugged her back just as tightly. Lily can fix what's broken simply by walking into a room, and I clung to her exuberant affection like the lifeline to sanity that it was.

"I'm so happy to see you, Claire-bear!" she said once she finally pulled back to assess me. "It's so good to...oh no! What's wrong?!"

That's how close we are. We're like sisters, so it wasn't surprising that in a two-second look, she'd been able to figure out something wasn't quite right. I didn't bother trying to deny it, either.

"You know how in professional car races when one car wrecks and flips, and then cars behind it can't avoid slamming into it, and pretty soon there's this stack of flaming cars with drivers jumping out of them to save their lives?"

"Um...sure?"

"That's how my life is going at the moment. Just like that."

"What?!" she cried, grabbing my arm and dragging me over to the couch. "Talk. You're on the Tell-a-Lily Hotline now."

"Mostly I just miss you I guess," I started.

"I miss you, too," she replied. "I'm sorry things have been so crazy lately."

"Oh, no, it's no one's fault, least of all yours. But it sucks. And work sucks, and I'm no closer to figuring out what I want to do about that. And then I went over to my mom's the other night. Chad was there, and I somehow ended up telling them that I told you about the dumb things he said about you."

"Claire!" she shrieked. "Why would you dredge that up again? Oh my gosh, I'm so embarrassed!"

"Yeah, that's basically what Chad said. I'm *so* sorry, Lils. He tore me apart over it, saying he never would have wanted to hurt your feelings like that, and that I had no business telling you those things in the first place. I can see now, with my hindsight goggles on, that he was right. I'm so sorry. You know I'd never try to hurt you on purpose. I swear I thought I was doing the right thing."

"Yeah, you know it hurt my feelings," she said. "Of course it did. I felt so stupid, but if you hadn't told me those things, we wouldn't have been in the lobby that day we met Jake and Max. I never would have been depressed enough to follow your advice about finding a writing buddy. And Max and I never would have fallen in love. So you stop right there with whatever horrible things you're telling yourself or regrets you're having. Max is the love of my life, and you set the ball rolling that led to us finding each other. You're not the villain here; you're the hero!"

"Only you could turn that around so fast to being something positive," I told her, a weird giggle snorting out of me in the least-attractive way possible.

"Okay, so...is that it?" she went on. "A few regrets over hurting my feelings can't possibly equal your flaming-pile-of-racecars analogy."

I nodded. "I've been evicted."

"What?!"

"Yeah, no kidding. Say goodbye to my cute little apartment and my cute little independence and my adorable little pride. Before you texted, I was about to call my mom to ask if I could move home until I can find a new apartment."

"Why were you evicted though? That's crazy."

"Mrs. Anderson's son has a new baby," I said, shrugging. "He wants to move into the other side of the house and dropkick his own mother over here, into the little in-law suite."

"Oh my gosh, Claire, that just sucks," she said, but then her eyes popped wide. I could practically see the cartoon lightbulb turn on over her head.

"Uh-oh...what are you thinking?" I demanded. "I can almost hear you having big ideas over there."

"I think I have the perfect solution for everyone!" she announced in what could only be called a shriek. "Max and I want to move in together, but we both signed leases not all that long ago, before we met. You could take over my lease, and I could move in with him! I'd just leave whatever furniture and stuff you'd want or need, so it wouldn't be much different than this place.

Well, I think my rent's a little higher than yours though."

"Lils…I'd happily pick up some extra shifts to cover the difference! But you better ask Max about this first. Is he really going to want me next door? And are *you*, for that matter?"

"Are you serious right now?" she asked, that cute little line scrunching up on her forehead as she looked at me. "We've been looking for this kind of solution for a while now, so it's perfect. Max knows you're like a sister to me. Who would I trust more? And you'd seriously be doing us a favor here. I could even chip in on that extra rent, since you'd be helping our expenses to chop down so dramatically."

"You're not handing me a perfect landing spot *and* paying my rent, but I appreciate the offer," I said. "You're serious though? You sure you don't need to run this by him first?"

"I'm beyond serious," she said. "Start packing immediately, and I will too. I'm so excited! This solves all our problems, and we'll see each other more often, too! No more struggling to find girlfriend time."

I laughed. "You might want to run *that* part of it past Max, Lils. He doesn't know what he's getting into here."

"Girl, he's going to be thrilled, so stop worrying. Now that we've solved those problems, are there any others? Or did we put out the fires on that stack of burning cars?"

"Nope," I said, feeling lighter than I had in weeks. "I think that about covers it."

*   *   *

After Lily left, I pulled out my suitcases and got to work.

Chapter 11

Max's Perfect Solution

I AGONIZED OVER that text to my brothers for a ridiculously and embarrassingly long time. I'd erased it, reworded it, then erased it and reworded it again, dozens of times. What made it so challenging was that it needed to express a lifetime of remorse and love, yet also somehow had to include me inviting myself to cannonball into the middle of the lovestruck pool of bliss and coupledom in which they were both floating these days. Still, it was easier than placing two separate phone calls, so I kept working on it.

Finally, tons of drafts later, I arrived at a pile of words that expressed what I wanted to say as well as anything else I'd come up with. Which is to say it was fine, but not great.

Me: I'm sorry I flipped out on you guys. I'm sorry for everything that's happened since we were kids, to be honest. The video call shocked me, and it's just taken a while to process it, I guess. But I'd like for us to talk again if you guys can forgive me. I just re-signed a lease here, so this can't be permanent, but I'm thinking about coming to visit. Anyone want a grumpy roommate with a hair-trigger anger problem?

I read through it a few more times and then just hit SEND before letting myself think about it any further. No words were going to be perfect here, anyway. There's no way to apologize for abandoning them. I'd never be able to make any of that right, clearly. But a visit was a good step in the right direction, if they'd even have me at this point.

It wasn't long before Jake's response arrived. Apparently, his word-choosing skills are faster and better developed than mine.

Jake: Get your butt on a plane immediately, and we'll figure it out. Melody and I put our houses on the market recently. She wants to distance herself from all the bad memories that hers holds, and mine is too small for the three of us. The realtor is showing both houses, and we've started looking for something in the same school district so Liam doesn't have to switch. Long story, but no crashing at my place.

Me: No worries, brother. Happy for you and Melody. Those are a lot of big steps you're taking. You weren't kidding that you're serious about her.

A stab of regret knifed its way through me as I typed out that reply. My brother was creating this whole new family with people I'd met just once. One more piece of painful evidence that demonstrated precisely how estranged I'd allowed myself to become.

Jake: Beyond serious, man. I want to ask her to marry me, but she wants us to wait until at least a full year after Dan's death before even talking about it. She doesn't want to embarrass his parents, basically.

Me: That's nice of her.

Jake: She's a beautiful person. You're going to love her.

Max: Mitch! I'm so glad you're finally coming, you jackwagon.

The arrival of Max's lighthearted text in the middle of all of that seriousness made me laugh out loud in the quiet of my apartment. I not only appreciated that he was being so forgiving, but also that he was trying to lighten the mood.

Me: Lol.

Max: And guess what? It's Max to the rescue, because I have the perfect solution. Lily and I re-signed our leases right before we met, but now we want to move in together. Why don't you stay in Lily's apartment, and she can move in with me? You coming here will give us some time to find someone to take over the lease.

Me: Yeah that'd really help me out, man. Although not sure I could afford to float both rents.

Max: We're paying for both apartments now anyway, so that doesn't need to change. Consider it the same as using our guest room.

I was blown away by his words. The loving forgiveness he was demonstrating in that generous offer was almost more than I could wrap my mind around. I didn't deserve any of it, that much I knew.

Me: I don't even know what to say to you, bro. Aren't you two neighbors? You sure you want that much of me all up in your face after all these years?

Max: We've got a lot of time to make up for, so shut up and start packing. Lily's over at Claire's right now. But when she gets home, we'll start figuring out a plan for getting her moved in, although half her junk is here anyway.

Me: Guess I've got a ticket to buy. Who wants to pick me up at the airport?

Jake: OMG you're high maintenance.

Me: Love you too, bro.

Jake: Just kidding. Glad you're on your way. Part of me has been missing for a long, long time.

Me: Me too.

Suddenly I felt like I couldn't wait another minute to be with my brothers again. I wasn't even sure how

I'd survived without them for so long. Excitement—not to mention relief—rattled through me. I pulled up the tab where I'd been eyeing flight prices for weeks, and I refreshed the search.

I found a decent-ish price on an upcoming flight, which forced me to push my departure back a couple of days. Disappointing, but it would give me time to finish up all the tasks that needed doing before abandoning my life in California for an undetermined amount of time. I hadn't thought about where to leave my car, for example, so I still had those kinds of problems to solve. But reaching out to my brothers and being met with nothing but welcoming kindness and love began to fix a lot of what was broken inside me. With those kinds of happy thoughts in my brain for a change, I bought the ticket and then went to analyze how bad my dirty-laundry situation had become so I could start packing. *Things are about to get a whole lot better for the Cruz brothers,* I thought as I dug around in my closet.

At least for this one, anyway.

Chapter 12

Moving Day

I WAS OFF the following day anyway, so I managed to pack my every worldly possession in record time, even factoring in the hour or two I wasted scrounging up some empty boxes at a few nearby businesses. I didn't need many, though. Like I said before, I didn't own much. I don't collect anything or have a bunch of complicated hobbies, although I may or may not have packed an entire box of nothing but chips.

It wasn't even dinnertime when I stacked the last box near the doorway. Other than emptying out the fridge and grabbing a few final toiletries from the bathroom, I was ready to roll. I hoped I wasn't moving too fast for Lily, I thought as I pulled out my phone to send her an update.

Me: I hope Max really was okay with all of this, because I spent the day packing. A couple of trips back and forth in my car should pretty much do it, I think.

Lily: Okay, good. Keep that vibe, and we'll be there to help soon, although I have some news you're not going to like.

Me: Girl, if Max doesn't want me moving in next door, just tell me straight out. This pile of crap can relocate to mom's house just as easily as your place, and you know I won't be mad at you about it.

Lily: Max said no such thing and never would. Chill out and hang on. We'll be there soon, and I promise it'll work out!

I felt a little guilty that I was maybe pressing too hard. But once I decide stuff, I'm ready to execute it. We agreed that I'd move into her old place, so I wanted it to happen in a snap—*poof!* Yup, impatience mixed with tactless honesty is what I bring to the table. No wonder so many people can't stand me.

When Lily got there, she wasn't alone. Both Max and Jake were trailing behind her, and everyone looked a little sheepish.

"Okay, first of all, you guys really didn't have to come help with this," I said. "I could have managed alone in a few trips."

"We sort of got volun-told to be here," Jake replied with a lazy smirk, "but you know we don't mind giving you a hand."

"P-plus we k-kind of owe you an apology," Max continued, eyeing my stack of boxes and suitcases. "Th-that's all you've g-got?"

"Yeah, I don't really own much. The apartment was furnished. But what do you mean you owe me an apology? An apology for what?"

"We kind of have a problem," Lily began. "And we're not exactly sure how to solve it without your help. While I was over here offering you the apartment, Max was home offering it to someone else."

"Oh...." I said, disappointment flooding through me. I hadn't realized how excited I was to move in next door to Lily until that very instant. "That sucks, but of course I understand. I won't stand in your way of giving it to someone else. Like I said, I'm sure my mom wouldn't mind me throwing all this junk in her garage while I apartment hunt."

"But that's the thing," Lily went on. "Having *you* move in is the better solution for us long-term, since you plan on fully taking over the lease, staying there for at least the rest of the year, and paying the rent on it."

I was utterly confused now. "Uh, okay, so who'd Max offer it to, then? Max, are you best friends with a squatter we don't know about?"

"Yeah," Jake said. "Squatter's name is Mitch."

Lily's eyes popped open. *"Nooo!* Why'd you blurt it out like that? We were gonna work our way up to it gently and butter her up for a while!"

"MITCH?!" I replied, my eyes even bigger than hers. "Your crazy-hot brother with the pro-level collection of red flags and anger issues? *That* Mitch?!"

"Uh, y-yeah?" Max said, looking a hundred times more sheepish now. "I kn-know it's j-just a one-bedroom, b-but maybe he c-could s-stay on the couch? He's just c-coming for a visit. N-nothing long term. Neither of us have any s-space for him, and I already t-told him he could s-stay there. I d-don't want to do anything to m-make him change his m-mind about coming."

"Wait—you guys don't think a cute little ray of sunshine like Mitch would get angry and dramatic about this mix-up, do you?" I asked, dropping my jaw open and putting my hand on my chest like I was clutching my pearls. No one does fake sarcasm as well as I do when I'm putting some effort into the performance.

"I mean, he *is* cute," Lily said, ignoring my floor show.

"Right?!" I said, pretending to fan myself.

"N-not this again!" Max said, rolling his eyes while Jake chuckled.

Lily was waving for my attention. "Claire, I'm sorry. I know we're putting you on the spot here, but unless we make him stay in a hotel—"

"...or, God forbid, he stayed with our mother—" Jake added.

"...then we're kind of in a bind," Lily finished, a pleading look on her face. "Pretty please?"

"Yeah, whatever," I replied after another moment. "I don't care if *he* doesn't. That's a big 'if' though. He didn't find me particularly charming, remember? Although with my crazy schedule lately, I'll barely be there anyway. So...seriously, whatever. And maybe we could chip in and buy a futon for the living room or something. I doubt a grown man is going to be comfortable on that doll-house size couch of yours, Lils."

"Oh yeah, that's a great idea!" she said. "Thank you so much! I knew you'd be cool with it!"

"No you didn't," I shot back, unable to miss the opportunity to tease her. "You just got done saying you thought you needed to butter me up first. You came in here all hot with that 'tame a wild horse' energy."

"I did, didn't I?" she said, giggling now as she opened her arms widely toward me. "Hugs!"

After Lily enclosed me in a vice-like hug for the ages, Jake said, "Okay, break it up you two." Then he grabbed a couple boxes. "Time to get moving. See what I did there?"

"H-hilarious, as always," Max added, grabbing the box with the chips in it. "This is so l-light. P-packed up that f-feather c-collection of yours?"

"Yes, I find them at all the major feather shows," I said, grabbing a couple suitcases and flashing Max a smile.

*   *   *

I really meant it when I told them I didn't mind if Mitch crashed with me for a while. Mostly—yes, I'm shallow like a puddle—he's pretty. Who *wouldn't* want to look at him every day? But part of me was interested in spending more time with him to see why he was already living rent-free in my head. I still had no idea why I'd been unable to get him off my mind since the video call.

Curious or not, though, I couldn't imagine he'd really stay with me anyway. Not after he found out about the double-booking. He had hated me on sight, even from a couple thousand miles away. I knew I was, at best, an acquired taste, even under normal circumstances. But Mitch was coming here to deal with a whole bunch of stressful family drama. Dealing with me was likely just about the last thing he needed.

Even I could admit that.

Chapter 13

Together Again

I DON'T KNOW WHY my nerves were eating me alive during the cross-country flight, or why I was just about crawling out of my skin with doubts and second-guesses as I stood on the curb with my suitcase, waiting for Jake to find me. I mean, yeah—of course I understood that it was weird being back home after so many years. But it was the interpersonal stuff that had my stress levels jumping. After all, I'd been a loner for a really long time. Probably not by nature, but I'd been forced to become one, and I'd been wearing that identity like armor. I guess it had mostly succeeded in protecting me. I had survived my years in exile, a few issues aside. But…yeah. I wasn't really used to being around people much.

Can I even DO this?

Worries that hadn't crossed my mind during my preparation for the trip were suddenly assaulting me like it was their full-time job. Was being swept up inside the hubbub that comes with a big family something I could tolerate? Because, yeah, with the addition of Melody, Liam, and Lily, we *were* becoming a pretty big family. How quickly would I wear out my welcome or, conversely, decide I needed to bolt?

Max's offer of an apartment of my own was looking better and better. If I got overwhelmed and had to put a little distance between myself and all that rampant togetherness I was about to join, I could retreat to the quiet solitude of Lily's old place.

That thought seemed to be the key to defusing my panic; I'd mostly stopped spiraling by the time a black pickup truck appeared, and Jake jumped out. He jogged around the back and was on the sidewalk before I could even move a muscle. When he reached the curb, I was standing there drinking in the sight of him with a dopey grin on my face. Loner or not, it sure was good to see him.

"It sure is good to see you, brother," Jake said, echoing my thoughts in the eerie way that he did sometimes. Maybe we hadn't completely broken our twin connection despite our years apart.

"I gotta confess, I was kind of tied in knots about being here," I told him. "But seeing you…it's good, bro."

The side of his mouth tugged up a little, like his brain couldn't quite decide if "sad" or "happy" was the appropriate response. I guess I could relate. Part of me was still jangling and worked up. Then again, simply standing there on an airport curb with him felt like a calm in my storm.

"Get over here," I said, leaning over and attempting one of those manly shoulder-thump things that pass as hugs. Then he grabbed me tighter and turned it into something with more force of feeling behind it.

"I'm sorry about that video call," he said, pulling back after a long moment. "I'm sorry about everything."

"Oh shut up," I replied, retreating from the regret in his eyes by grabbing my suitcase and hefting it into the truck's bed. "You know I'm the one who owes all the apologies in this family."

He gave me a rueful look, then headed back to the

cab. Soon we were strapped in and creeping through the traffic that New Jersey, like California, is known for.

We made a bunch of small talk on the drive to Max's apartment building. He told me more about how he and Melody met, and I learned that Liam's first word was "Jake" when he finally emerged from trauma-fueled silence that had stretched out for months. The situation was astonishingly similar to what Max had gone through, and I was also taken aback because that story showed me precisely what a good man my brother had become. While I'd been licking my wounds and hating the world, Jake had been busy saving it one traumatized boy at a time.

The realization didn't do a whole lot to steady those jangling nerves or worries that were taking up all that space in my head.

*   *   *

When I saw Max, he gave me a hug every bit as fierce as the one Jake had wrapped me into, and I could feel the forgiveness pouring out of both of them. Like my earlier realization about how much better a man Jake was than I could ever be, I was humbled by their easy acceptance and forgiveness.

"Where's Lily?" I asked after Max released me from his embrace. "Figured my old buddy would be here to see me."

They exchanged a not-very-subtle, totally worried glance, and my stomach twisted. *Now what?*

"Is she okay?" I asked. "You're freaking me out here."

"N-no, she's f-fine," Max said. "She's n-next door. Uh…with C-Claire."

"Claire?" I asked. "The barnacle on the side of our family video call? *That* Claire?"

As those words were coming out of my mouth, the door opened, and Lily and Claire walked in. The smirk on the latter's face made it clear that she'd heard my comment.

"Hey, look, it's me," she said, whipping out a low-energy set of jazz hands. "The barnacle!"

"Yaaayyyy," I said in a sarcastically weak tone. "We meet again."

"Oh, we're going to do more than just meet, my prickly friend," she replied, that annoying smirk still pasted on her annoying face.

"Work up to it!" Lily cried, smacking her face into her palm. "Oh my gosh! Doesn't anyone in this family know how to butter people up before dropping bad news?"

"Bad news?" I asked. "What's going on Lily?"

"Hugs first!" she said. "Oh Mitch, it's so good to see you again! You are the best guy in the world and one of my favorite people after the way you helped Max and me!" She pulled back from our hug before adding to the others, "See? That's how the pros do it!"

"Yup, that was some grade-A buttering," I assured her. "So come on. Let's have it. What's this news that I'm not going to like?"

"Uh, well, I kind of, sort of, offered Claire my apartment," she said, wincing. "I didn't know Max was going to offer it to you, too. We sort of did it simultaneously."

"What are you saying?" I asked, even though I had a pretty solid guess as to what was coming.

"Heeey roomie!" Claire said like she was greeting a long-lost sorority sister. "Surprise!"

And just like that, my visions of having my own space and a quiet retreat withered and died.

Chapter 14

Roommates

HE LOOKED LIKE a trapped animal about to chew its own leg off to escape. I knew I hadn't exactly made the best impression on him—I mean, the man *had* just compared me to a barnacle. But the look in his eyes held way too much force of emotion, and nothing about the moment was making sense to me. It wasn't an "Oh my gosh this chick's annoying" look I was seeing. No, it was more of a panicked "I don't think I can do this" kind of thing.

I wasn't the only one who seemed to realize Mitch was teetering on the edge of hopping right back on a plane. Lily's face was a neon sign lit up with worry. Max and Jake were both upset and exchanging nervous looks, too. Overall, we seemed sort of frozen in the anticipation of just how destructive and far-reaching the inevitable shockwaves from his reaction would be.

As much as I love my girl, it wasn't necessarily all that worry from Lily and her man that was getting to me as much as it was the pain in his eyes. I still thought he was a jerk they'd be better off without, but something about that look made me want to try to throw myself on top of the bomb and shelter them all from the explosion.

"Hey, listen," I said. "Although you've been crazy subtle about it, I kind of get the idea that maybe you don't like me or something."

His lips quivered a bit, as though he was wrestling

back a smile—which was an improvement over the trapped-terror vibe—so I kept going.

"And you're not exactly a skip through the park to pick daisies yourself. So I'll prove I'm the better person here. I'll let you have the apartment while you're in Jersey, and I'll go stay with my mom. Then, when you leave, I'll reattach to the rest of your family barnacle-style. But you're not getting my box of Doritos and potato chips. That goes with me."

"The b-box of f-feathers was chips?" Max asked, chuckling now. "Seriously?"

"Don't chip-shame me, man," I replied. "So, what do you say? Will that make you whatever passes for happy in your grumpy little world?"

"Oh Claire!" Lily said. "I'm so sorry. You're being such a good sport to offer the apartment while he's here. We owe you one!"

"I'm awesome like that," I said. "Despite what some people think."

"No, you don't have to go," Mitch said, finally breaking his silence with a sigh and a roll of his eyes. "Sure, I mean, you *do* have the personality of a honey badger, but you kind of had me at Doritos."

"Keep the Doritos out of this," I said. "You're going to *think* honey badger if you touch my stash."

"Listen, it's been a long day," he said after an actual chuckle fell out of his mouth. "Shall we get out of everyone's hair and go figure this out?"

"Only if you're sure," I said, shrugging even as something inside me did a happy little cartwheel.

I was about to get my chance to try to get to know the big lug better. Maybe I could even figure out why I felt even more drawn to him in person than I had on that video call. And why I'd been ready to slink away from my new apartment without a fight just to ease his pain.

*   *   *

As Mitch grabbed his bag and made some sort of plan to join his brothers at the gym the next morning, Lily yanked me into the hallway.

"Oh my gosh, he was about to bolt, wasn't he?" she asked, her voice a low hiss.

"That's kind of what I thought, too," I said. "And I'm still not sure he's gonna stick around long."

"It just breaks my heart. Max and Jake want him back in their lives so desperately, and they were so excited about this visit. I'm just going to die if this stupid apartment mix-up is what kills it for them."

"Hey, I offered to leave," I reminded her. "He could have taken me up on it."

"I think he was just trying to be nice. So please, I'm begging you, try to make this work. Okay? If it looks like he's about to lose it again, do you mind making that offer to leave a second time?"

"Lils, come on. You know I'd do anything for you. But don't worry, I've got this. He's about to experience the true joy that is me."

She beamed at me as the door opened, and Mitch walked out.

"Ready?" he asked.

"Ready," I replied. After that I mouthed *I've got this* back to Lily, who gave me a little wave and mouthed *Thank you!* before disappearing back into Max's apartment.

Fishing out the key to "our" place, I unlocked the door and pushed it open. He walked in and set down his bag, then surveyed the small apartment.

"It's a one-bedroom?" he asked.

"Yeah, so here's the thing," I said. "Lily had some crazy idea that one of us could sleep on the couch, but come on, look at that thing. *Liam* would find it restrictive."

"Great."

"So, I was thinking we could share the bed tonight and go buy a futon to throw out here in the living room tomorrow. I mean, it'll eat up the entire room if the Barbie couch stays, but who cares, right?"

"You serious right now? The two of us? Share a bed tonight?"

"Well, now, relax Sparky, because my offer to go to my mom's still stands. So feel free to tell me to leave. But I figured what's the big deal with one night? Unless…wait, are you scared that I'll barnacle onto you, too?"

"Yeah, um….sorry about that barnacle thing."

"No you're not," I told him. "But that's okay. You have to work harder than that to hurt my feelings. So which way are we playing this? Be truthful now. Want me to leave? I promise it's not a biggie."

I almost laughed at the puzzled look on his face as he assessed me for a few seconds.

"I swear I can't figure you out," he said finally. "But I don't want to look like any more of a jerk to my brothers than I already do. So please stay. I'm begging you to help me out here. Help me pretend, for their sakes, that I'm an easygoing guy who can roll with things."

"Sure, I can help you create that illusion," I replied, nodding. "And I'll even try to keep my hands off you tonight."

At that comment he actually laughed, and I was

treated to the first genuinely lighthearted look I'd ever seen on his face. *Heaven help me,* I thought. Because that smile made him look even more beautiful than he had looked before.

And that was saying a *lot.*

Chapter 15

Comfortable

WHEN HAD I TURNED into such an inflexible grouch? Only I could have sent sweet Lily and my brothers into a panic over something as simple as a forced roommate situation. And they'd been right to panic about my reaction, because I'd been about two seconds from calling a car service to take me back to the airport when Claire jumped in with her offer to leave. Once she threw it out there and made herself look like a freaking saint, I'd had no choice but to suck it up and pretend to be cool with it.

I mean, it wasn't really Claire herself—although I swear I couldn't figure out what in the world Lily got out of the friendship with her—but more that I just wasn't going to have anywhere to hide when the family dynamics became too much to take. What if the doctors said it was time to pull the plug on the old man, and all my secrets started beating on the doors of their prison inside me, clamoring to be set free? I'd need time alone with my worries and doubts to think it all over and decide what to do. Time I wasn't going to get now, not without the company of a certain hostile roommate.

Speaking of that hostile roommate, she let me take my turn in the bathroom first, where I showered off and slid into a pair of sweats and a t-shirt. Then we switched and she took her turn, silence accompanying our uneasy choreography.

It struck me then that there was something so

strangely familiar about her. That, of course, made no sense though. Her snarky comments and constant, unfiltered honesty were so unique. I seriously didn't even know what to make of her; she was so utterly different from any person—man or woman—I'd ever met. On the other hand, for as much as she was a total stranger to me and someone who I couldn't really figure out, being around her didn't feel all that uncomfortable. It was almost like we'd rehearsed this all before. Being with her felt…I guess I'll say it again: familiar. Easy, even, although that couldn't be right, could it? She was so prickly; how could sharing an apartment and a bed with her feel *easy?*

Exhaustion made me stop trying to analyze it, and we climbed into bed quietly, not even stopping to discuss which side we preferred. We somehow reached a silent agreement, got settled, and then she turned out the light.

"G'night, Mitch," she said casually, as if this were the most normal thing that had happened to her all week.

"G'night, Honey Badger," I said, smiling into the dark when I heard her short, answering cackle.

*　　　*　　　*

I'm not known for my deep, restful sleep. As when I'm conscious, I never seem to find peace at night, either. Often unhappy memories turn into equally unhappy dreams, sending me, thrashing and fitful, into another day of my tired existence. But not that night. I guess the exertion involved in dealing with all my anxieties about the trip had finally caught up with me, because I slept harder and deeper than I ever remember doing before. No bad dreams. No fitful tossing. Just sleep.

When I fuzzily rose back into consciousness, I slowly realized two things. The first was that I felt better than I probably had in years. The second was that I was currently wrapped around Claire like a human blanket.

Part of me was horrified and embarrassed, but the well-rested side of me was too comfortable to care. I didn't think she was awake yet, so I decided not to make any hasty moves; I mean, so I wouldn't wake her up and stuff. I tried not to think about things like how soft her skin was or how sweet she looked in sleep, when she wasn't being defensive and snarky. Actually, I was in so much deep thought about it that I didn't notice right away when her eyes fluttered open, and I jumped a little when she spoke.

"Oh my gosh, you're so warm!" she said, kind of snuggling into me now. Guess she wasn't mad. And I guess I wasn't the only one who was too comfortable to notice how weird this was. "I am literally always cold," she went on. "And yes, I understand the power that the word 'literal' packs into that sentence, but I'm serious. I'd be cold in a hot tub inside a forest fire. But you're like an electric blanket."

"Uh, sorry," I said, mentally high fiving her for her accurate word analysis—*Take that, Tifanee!*—and peeling away from her. I decided to ignore the weird feeling that sort of seemed like regret jogging through me as I rolled away. "I don't remember flopping all over you last night, and I definitely didn't mean to invade your personal space. So, seriously, I'm sorry. Won't happen again. You know, futon plans and whatever."

"Who's the barnacle now?" she said, ignoring my rambling as another laugh that could only be called a cackle burst out of her. So much for her looking sweet.

"But seriously, I didn't mind. I wasn't kidding about always being cold."

"I must not have minded either," I told her, "because that was the best sleep I think I've ever gotten. Guess I really crashed hard after the build-up of emotions it took to get myself here."

She looked like she wanted to ask me more about that, but I could see the moment she talked herself out of it. Looked like maybe I wasn't the only one off-balance. There we were, two strangers who didn't particularly like each other, lying in bed chatting like old friends. It made no sense. Of course, not much made sense in my life, so what did one more bit of confusion matter?

"Want the bathroom first?" she asked, stretching now. "I might have heard you agree to go to the gym with your brothers, and I think they go pretty early."

"Yeah, thanks," I said as I got out of the bed and headed for the bathroom, trying to shake off this weird situation with Claire. I couldn't be worrying about my odd roommate or about the fact that things with her should be weirder than they actually were. What I really needed to focus on was spending time with my brothers—and deciding how many of my secrets I should set free.

Chapter 16

Post-Panini Debriefing

THE BROTHERS HAD barely walked down the hall toward the elevator when Lily showed up at my door looking like she'd vaporize if I didn't feed the gossip machine.

"Please tell me things went well last night!" she said, stopping to squeeze me into a tight embrace. Then she looked around as if she thought a full night of nothing but Mitch and me might require some crime scene tape, chalk outlines, and witness statements.

"I *told* you I had this under control," I replied, mostly—but not entirely—confident in my words. "Everything was fine, so relax."

"Really?" Her face wrinkled into an accordion of doubt. "You? And Mitch? The two of you? Together? Here? And there were *zero* problems?"

"I'm offended you'd even think that," I sniffed in a totally fake show of indignation.

"He thinks you're a leech on the side of the Cruz family. So yeah, I was worried."

"Barnacle," I said. "Come on, keep up. But, yes, it was fine. We came over here, took turns in the bathroom, got into bed, said goodnight, spooned like that couple that goes down with the ship in the *Titanic* movie, and then he got up and left. Seriously, it was almost exactly like what you probably thought would happen."

"WHAT???!!!" she screeched in a tone sure to get

neighborhood dogs howling. "You…something *happened* with you two? I asked you to smooth things over, not sleep with him! What happened to him crashing on the couch?"

"Would you listen to yourself here?" I said. "We can't *stand* each other, and he's way too hot to notice me anyway. We didn't sleep together—we *slept* together. Just for one night until we can get that futon we talked about. Come on, no one was going to get any sleep on your Lego couch."

"Well, okay…sounds harmless enough, I suppose. But what about the spooning? You were joking, right?"

"Oh, no, that part happened," I said, shrugging as her eyes bugged out of her face. Truth was, I couldn't exactly explain it to her since I couldn't make sense of it myself. The whole thing had been simultaneously the weirdest and also the most comforting experience in my life. "I don't know. At some point I guess he rolled over and scooped me up. It was like sleeping inside a panini press."

She still looked flabbergasted. "Huh. Okay, so, do you think you guys are going to…get together?"

How nice that she lived in a sparkling world of make-believe where someone as mega-hot as Mitch would even notice that I'm female. "Lily, darling, sweet Lily. I know you love me, so you see me through rosy glasses. But there's no way that would ever happen. He's a *model!* He's a muscle-bound, tattoo-covered female fantasy. Plus, there's the whole issue of the mutual disdain we've got going on. His nickname for me is 'Honey Badger.' That doesn't scream hot romance, Lils."

"Claire, this isn't simply friendship talking," she said, love for me emanating from each word. Whatever childhood circumstances led to us bonding tight on the playground during third-grade recess were the best things that ever happened to me. "You're beautiful, inside and out. It's not you being worthy of him that's the problem, it's the fact that he seems so utterly broken. It's especially obvious when you compare him to Jake. They look so much alike, but the similarities seem to end there. Jake is kind and selfless and giving, but it sort of seems like Mitch only cares about Mitch."

"Yeah, true, the comparison with Jake does make him seem like even more of a hot mess than he already did. Don't forget he's hiding something from his brothers. Who knows, but he might be even more of a dumpster fire than we already think."

"It's so sad. The whole situation makes me want to cry."

"Well, I just hope Max and Jake don't get hurt in the. fallout. I think if my roomie ever detonates and releases his secret, things might get even more painful for all of them. Who knows what he's hiding?"

Lily's face drooped into a sad frown that pretty much summed up the situation perfectly. But hey, what did it matter to me, right? Mitch's accusations aside, I wasn't *actually* attached to their family. Their reality-TV drama meant nothing to me.

*   *   *

Despite telling myself it wasn't my problem, our discussion stayed with me all day, right through another exhausting shift. They really needed to hire more servers, but the turnover had been brutal lately. I guess it was good for me, though. I was working long hours, which would help me with my increased-rent situation. It would also help keep me away from the apartment so Mitch and I wouldn't have to interact much.

Part of me would cheerfully seek any excuse to stay as far away from him as possible while he was in Jersey, but I'd be lying if I didn't keep thinking about how strangely amazing it felt to wake up in his arms. Yes, it was warm. But it had been more than that, too. I woke up feeling…safe, I guess. Comforted, even. Mostly I felt—just for my few seconds of awareness before he pulled away—like I wasn't so alone. And yes, I know none of those feelings made sense. Comforted? By freaking Mitch, the walking caution sign?

But I meant what I'd said to Lily—there was no way anything could ever happen between the two of us under any circumstances. I couldn't possibly be his type. That was sort of the heart of what made me worry I'd be alone forever, with or without the Mitch Factor. I was starting to suspect I wasn't *anyone's* type, and I felt kind of down about it in general. The junk with Sebastian simply had been more proof in my already-enormous stack of evidence that maybe I just wasn't cut out to be in a long-term relationship. Who in the world would want to deal with me and my inability to censor myself? No one, I'm pretty sure.

So I got through the day and might have even spent a handful of minutes not thinking about my strange roommate situation. Actually, it wasn't until I was walking through the lobby of the apartment building that evening that I remembered what I'd totally forgotten.

Futon shopping….

Which meant I'd be spending another night in the panini press. And when I pushed the button for the elevator, I suddenly realized I had a smile on my face.

Chapter 17

Bedside Confession

"HOW'D IT GO with Claire last night?" Jake asked when Max and I joined him at the gym. "I'm going to guess it wasn't too bad since it looks like you actually got some sleep."

"Yeah, you know, spending time with her isn't exactly a dream scenario," I told him, "but honestly it was fine. I slept like a baby."

"G-got up every th-three hours crying for a b-bottle?" Max asked. I chuckled, kind of astonished. I'd forgotten how funny he could be.

"Yes, that's right. Once I found my pacifier, I was out like a light."

Then Jake introduced me to a few of his surprised coworkers, and it seemed I wasn't the only subpar communicator. No one had any idea I even existed before his introduction. That didn't make me feel too great, although I knew I would've done the same thing. Maybe the whole not-talking-about-each-other thing made our separation hurt less. Or maybe it just helped bury that pain more deeply. It was probably that kind of clever emotional management that landed Jake in the hospital in the first place. So yeah, maybe we needed to up our communication games a bit.

Of course, that was ironic coming from me, the secret vault. And speaking of that vault, I should have known that my brothers weren't going to forget that I'd messed up during our video call when I verbally tripped over myself and accidentally revealed that I was carrying around a secret about Dad. It wasn't long before they jumped into that topic with both feet.

"When are you g-going to tell us wh-what you're hiding?" Max asked. We were on the stair climbers, and I was impressed that our baby brother wasn't even winded. In fact, he was very physically fit. I'd known that Jake had been dragging him to the gym for years, but I guess I'd never seen the effects until just then. Of course, that was just a drop in the ocean of what I'd missed in total.

"Who says I'm hiding anything?" I asked, trying out the classic play-dumb defense.

"You did, you idiot," Jake fired back. "You did everything but advertise it in Times Square on that video call. You know you did, so stop playing dumb."

Again, he'd echoed my thoughts. I was so happy we still seemed connected, and I couldn't help responding with a big, cheesy smile.

"What?" he asked. "Why are you making that dopey face?"

"No reason. This is just nice. The three of us here together like this."

"Right. It's awesome, and we want it to stay like this. So stop changing the subject, which—in case you forgot already—is what are you hiding?"

"I…I can't say," I replied slowly. "Not yet. I need to see the old man first. I need to *know.*"

"Know wh-what?" Max asked.

I sighed. "That he's really not going to wake up, because he…he's the reason." My words were limp and lame compared with the enormity of the truth they held.

"He's the reason for what?" Jake asked, stopping

his machine and swinging a razor-edged glare my way. "Talk to us! He's the reason for *what?*"

"He's the reason I left," I said, also stopping and grabbing my towel. "Come on, it doesn't take a veteran detective to figure that much out. You guys had to have known that's why I left."

"Of course we d-did," Max said, furiously maintaining his pace for a few seconds longer before coming to a halt. "And you j-just admitted that's no s-secret. But you *are* k-keeping a secret, s-something you specifically s-said you were t-trying to hide from *me*. S-so what is it, M-Mitch? What's the r-rest of the story?"

"I'm serious here," I said, taking a drink of water to stall a few seconds while I gathered my thoughts. "I need to see the old man first. Max, have *you* seen him yet?"

"N-no, I haven't s-seen him in years."

"After I left, but before you were able to move out, did things…did it get better for you?" I asked. "Did he finally lay off?"

"I guess so. H-he seemed to l-lose interest in anything to d-do with me. Why do you ask? Is th-that somehow r-related to your leaving?"

"Jake, what's your work schedule like today?" I asked, letting Max's question float away unanswered. "And how about you, Max? Do you guys have time to go to the hospital with me?"

"I'm f-freelance," Max said. "I m-make my own hours."

"And I moved my schedule around when I found out you were coming," Jake added. "So I'm free too."

"Guess we're doing this then," I told them. "Well, Max, if you even want to join us in the first place. You've been purposely avoiding him since you found out about the coma, right?"

"Yeah. That's b-been a survival s-skill of mine for years. But I suppose I n-need to face him one l-last time."

And that's how the three of us ended up standing around his bed, looking into the withered face of the man who'd almost single-handedly—not to downplay Mom's role—destroyed our family.

*   *   *

He looked frail, powerless, and shriveled. It was so startling that I had a moment of panic, like I couldn't get enough air in my chest. I struggled for a few endless seconds before finally managing to drag in a jagged gasp of air, startling both of my brothers.

"You okay?" Jake asked, his worry wrapping around me as I weakly nodded my head, my eyes still locked on that nightmarish figure in the bed. "I know it's a lot to take in. How about you, Maxwell? You okay?"

"N-no," he said, looking every bit as shaken as I felt. This man's anger and hatred had been so big that it couldn't even be contained inside that singular body. His venomous nature had grown and expanded and spread its tentacles into every aspect of our lives. Seeing the pitiful remnants of all that darkness was…I don't even know the right word. Frustrating? Infuriating? I mean, really, how *dare* he steal our happy childhoods and try to break the bonds that knit us together?

Suddenly the rage I felt couldn't be contained inside me any more successfully than he'd been able to hold in his own anger. *Condemn me to a life of loneliness just so I could keep his stupid secrets and protect his misplaced pride? Screw that….*

"He blackmailed me into leaving," I blurted out.

That statement—which caused my brothers to

swing matching looks of shock my way—marked the first crack in my vault of secrets. Unfortunately for me, it didn't help to release any of my anger. And it sure didn't take away my pain.

Chapter 18

Not Family

GOOFY HOPES about another warm night spent snuggling inside a certain hostile interloper's toasty arms propelled me out of the elevator and down the hall to my door. As much as I loved this new apartment and all the Lily-access it offered, I missed parking in Mrs. Anderson's driveway, which was only a few steps from my door.

I was so lost in all that musing that I almost gasped in shock when I walked in to find almost the entire Cruz family assembled in my living room. Well, I didn't see Liam, but the rest of the gang was there.

"I guess you're all wondering why I invited you here tonight," I said, trying for a joke, even though what I really wanted to know was why this...whatever it was...had to be happening here. In *my* space, and at the end of *my* freakishly long day. Didn't any of these people have homes of their own where they could hold secret meetings? Like literally next door, for example?

"Sorry!" Lily said, jumping up to hug me. "Mitch dropped a bomb on his brothers today and then tried to retreat into his cave of isolation. But as you can see, that didn't work out so well for him."

"Huh," I replied, struggling to process her words and the emotionally charged looks I could read on everyone's faces. "Guess no one wants to hear about the party of ten I served today that gave me a five-dollar tip, huh?"

"You're a waitress?" Mitch asked, making no effort to hide the amusement he found in that piece of information. What a jerk. "You not getting big tips totally tracks."

"Yes, Mitch, I'm a waitress. Would you like a side of fries with your condescension? And last I heard, you're not exactly solving world hunger yourself."

"Sorry," he lobbed back with what sounded like minimal sincerity. "Didn't mean anything by it. But please tell me you bought that futon today."

"Nope. Which part of my sentence about working today confused you? I'm a waitress, and no I don't work at the snack bar in Futons-to-Go. So I couldn't grab one on my break and strap it to the top of my Corolla."

"Would you two chill out?" Jake said. "We were in the middle of a family summit, remember? Focus. Mitch, you were about to tell us what you meant when you said that Dad blackmailed you into leaving. All you did was drop that bomb, but obviously there's more to the story. Come on. We're all family here. Talk to us."

"*She's* not family," Mitch said, jabbing an accusatory finger in my direction. "And I don't have anything more I want to say right now anyway. Give me time, man."

"We gave you time," Jake went on. "Years and years of time."

Lily shot me a pleading look that I immediately understood. My role in all of this was to offer up my living room along with my absence. All in the name of protecting a group of people to whom I did not belong. So it was very clear where I stood.

"Well, on that note, I guess I'll go take a shower," I announced. "Don't worry, I haven't had a chance to plant any bugs in here yet, so you're free to spill your family secrets without getting my nasty non-family grossness all over you."

Lily mouthed *Sorry!* at me, but I just winked at her and disappeared into my room as quickly as I could shove through the Cruz family war council, all seated in chairs they'd pulled out of the kitchen.

Gee, if only we had a futon, I thought.

*   *   *

I was showered and tucked into bed when Mitch finally knocked at the door, only peeking in when I replied that he could enter.

"Can I still sleep in here, or did my nastiness toward you make me lose privileges?"

"Nah, climb aboard," I told him. Not gonna lie— despite what a jerk he was, I was still hoping for a repeat of the panini situation.

He got in bed, tucking his arms under his head as he stared at the ceiling, lost in thought about whatever truths his brothers had managed to drag out of him, no doubt.

"I'm sorry," he said, finally breaking the silence. "I might have a teensy problem with lashing out in anger when I feel backed into a corner. And there was some high-energy corner-backing happening out there."

"I know that. I might be a bit of a corner-lasher myself, so I understand."

"Just because I know you can take it doesn't mean you deserve it though. None of this crap has anything to do with you, so you certainly don't need to get beat up over it."

"Oh, yeah, I may have picked up on your feelings about whether or not I should be involved," I told him. "I'm good at reading between the lines."

He chuckled softly, then turned his head so he was looking at me.

"Didn't mean to sound judgey about your job, either. The vision of you working daily in customer service just kind of struck me as funny."

I laughed; I mean, come on, he wasn't wrong.

"Yeah, well...you *did* hear the part about me not getting a great tip today, right? Meekly serving mouthy people probably isn't my life's calling."

"What *is* your life's calling, then?" he asked, turning his gaze back toward the ceiling. "You going to school or something?"

"I got a generic bachelor's in communication," I said, utterly confused why I was opening up to him but unable to stop the words from falling out of my mouth. "I graduated, but I can't figure out what career I want. I'm not someone like Melody, with her lifelong dream of being a vet. I'm...kind of lost, to be honest."

"Me too," he replied, so softly that I barely heard him.

"Modeling isn't your dream job?"

"Oh, no, it's fine. It pays the bills for now, and even though it's not solving world hunger, as you pointed out, I'm pretty good at it. Eventually I can do personal training, like Jake, if I want to branch out. It's not the job that's the problem."

"It's all the interpersonal stuff, then?"

"Yeah. I know you heard the update about what I told my brothers."

"Your dad blackmailed you. So how'd he manage to do that?"

"He knew I'd do anything in the world to protect my brothers. And he was right."

"I'm sorry," was all I said in response. There were

a billion follow-up questions I could have asked, but I reminded myself that I wasn't his family, and I sure wasn't his friend. Several long minutes passed by, and eventually he fell asleep.

I turned away from him and tried to do the same thing. I was cold and a little restless for most of the night, but eventually Mitch rolled over and pulled me into his arms again, surrounding me in his warmth.

And for the second night in a row, we both slept deeply, cocooned tightly together.

Chapter 19

Snuggler

I DID IT AGAIN. Two nights in a row I slept better than I can remember, and that includes those times when I'm knocked out on cold medicine. Either that mattress was made from angel tears, or my new champion sleep skills had something to do with Claire, the enigma who was wrapped up tightly in my arms. But come on, that made no sense. She and I were so combustible together. What about her would possibly soothe or comfort me?

But something *had* to be doing exactly that, because a million worries and problems were swirling nonstop in my head. The fact that I was getting any sleep at all was a miracle, but to be sleeping deeply and well? Like I said before, it's just not what I've ever been capable of, so I didn't know to what I owed my good fortune. But I knew one thing for certain—I didn't want it to end.

My brothers, along with Melody and Lily to some extent, had tried so hard to get me to talk the night before, but I was stressed out and utterly uncertain how to handle any of it. Was it time to tell them everything after all these years? I was convinced, after that hospital visit, that our dad wouldn't be leaping up and accusing me of breaking any deals in the near future. And likely never again. So no, it wasn't looking like he needed to be a factor in any of my decision making, and he certainly shouldn't be the reason I kept all my truths bottled up inside me.

Beyond the deal with my father, the other reason I'd remained locked in silence for years had to do with Max and his well-being. But even after a single day in his company, I was convinced his turnaround was real and permanent. No setbacks were going to send him flying off the cliff and back into the trauma of silence that had imprisoned him for years. Nothing about his demeanor yesterday seemed timid or unsure. And he and Lily were absolutely crazy about each other, so there were no worries there. Her love and support seemed like they would be his anchor in any storm.

*   *   *

When Claire began mumbling in her sleep, I felt a flutter of guilt—*I really should get my hands off her.* But the truth of the matter was that I *liked* having her in my arms, and that truth was just one more log on the fires of confusion burning nonstop in my brain. We couldn't stand each other, and I wasn't exactly known for my top-shelf cuddling skills, even under normal circumstances. Honestly, I'd never allowed myself to get close enough to any woman to reach the stage of wanting to lounge around in each other's arms as we whispered nighttime confidences. I don't think I'd even had Tifanee over to my apartment. I either went to her place or we went out somewhere.

Suddenly I realized Claire was awake and peering over her shoulder at me.

"What are you thinking about so hard over there?" she asked, snuggling deeper into my arms.

"How I'm absolutely not—and have never been—the snuggling type," I replied.

"I don't know, Mitch. I think we've uncovered a whole new career for you. Turns out you're an amazing snuggler. The best, really. I have never been so warm in my life."

"This is so weird. *We* are so weird together."

"Oh, come on. Lighten up. We're just making the best of an odd situation, but I don't think we're innately weird, together or apart."

"We can't get along for two straight minutes during the daytime, but I've never slept this well at night," I pointed out. "Seriously. Ever."

"Want to know my theory?" she asked, rolling around now to look at me. Being that close to her, our faces mere inches apart, felt way too intimate, so I let go of her and rolled onto my back. I'll admit it: I missed the feel of her in my arms the second I let her go.

"You have a theory?" I asked, fighting the urge to pull her to me again. "I'd love to hear it, because I've currently got nothing but questions, problems, and confusion."

"Okay you asked for it. So, you're here with your family for the first time in years. Everyone desperately needs you, and they want so much for you to dump all your secrets and hang ups, kick them to the side, and walk straight back into the family fold. It's too much pressure. You've spent years being on your own and hiding a bunch of stuff from them. You don't know who you are anymore without that cloak of solitude. You don't want to let them all down, but you're not ready to lift them all up, either. It's a ton of pressure. Pressure, pain, and self-doubt."

I nodded. "That makes sense. But it doesn't explain...this." I did a back-and-forth gesture between us since I couldn't find the words to explain our situation.

"Yeah, I'm getting to that part," she said. "So, here I am, the only person around right now who has no expectations of you. Actually, I kind of have *negative* expectations of you, if I'm being honest. I don't need you, I don't know you, and I'm not even sure I like you. So you're grabbing onto the one person you can't let down, like the calm in your storm and the sanity in your crazy. Why do you think you've told me about a billion times that I'm not part of your family? You don't *need* more family right now. And you really don't want me caught up in all that pressure you're under. What you like about being with me is that I'm just…nothing to you, I guess."

"No, you're not…." I started, then trailed off because I was unable to form a coherent response. "You're…okay, look, you're not *nothing* to me. And actually, wow, I'm…uh, blown away by you right now, I guess. Maybe counseling is your life's calling? Because that might have been the deepest thing anyone's ever said about me."

"Yeah, but how deep are the people you hang out with?" she asked, teasing in her voice. "From what I know of you, that might have been a veiled insult."

"Well, yeah, you got me; I confess I'm not super deep," I admitted with a chuckle. "I broke up with a woman recently, largely because she misused the word 'literally' all the time. Drove me absolutely crazy. And her name was Tifanee, but she spells it weird, involving way too many 'e's. I just couldn't take it."

Claire laughed until tears were streaming down her face, which then made me laugh, too. I've never really been a morning person, but lying there laughing with her was the best time I'd had in a really long time.

"I was dumped recently, too," she said when she finally regained control of herself. "I don't think the word 'literally' was a factor, though."

"What was?" I asked, not able to resist. "Your

sunny demeanor was just too much positivity for him?"

"Hah!" she said. "C'mon, you know the reason. He said I don't have any tact. I mean, just because I told him his constant, stupid fantasy football talk was boring."

"Guess I should have asked you if you were seeing anyone before this whole shared-bed situation came up, huh?" I was unwilling to analyze why a surge of relief went through me when she said she was single. *Or, wait—is she?* "Or did you start seeing someone new in the meantime?"

"Nah," she said. "That all happened right before you arrived. It's not like I've got a waiting list."

There was no mistaking it that time. When she confirmed she was single, relief definitely did a victory lap through my chest. What was *that* about? The last thing I needed was to get involved with someone right now, and certainly not one of Lily's best friends. When I inevitably took off from here and ended things in a month or two or whatever, being involved with a woman would add a whole extra layer of complication that my family drama definitely didn't need. Plus, Claire had just gotten done saying she wasn't even sure she liked me. So there was no way we'd be walking any further down this imaginary path.

"You got any plans today?" I asked, deciding to end the craziness permanently. "Want to go futon shopping?"

An odd look flickered across her face. I wasn't sure if it was hurt or regret. But she simply nodded her head.

"Okay, yeah, let's go futon shopping."

"Excellent."

There.... I'd put an end to whatever this situation was between us. And when I eventually got a great night's sleep on the futon, totally alone, I'd prove that my new ability to sleep and find peace had absolutely nothing to do with Claire.

94

Chapter 20

The Futon

LYING IN BED with Mitch and laughing that morning had made me feel closer to him than I'd ever felt to any guy. *Ever.* Which, I guess, now that I'm saying it out loud, is sort of sad.

But it also gives as clear a picture of my dating history as anything else, so I'll pretend it's really okay. Anyway, I'm not going to lie; it kind of hurt when he suddenly was dying to go find that freaking futon. I was sort of hoping—between the laughter and the warmth—that we could just keep going with our little arrangement. It was mutually beneficial, after all, right? Didn't he say being in bed with me was giving him the best sleep of his life?

Maybe sleep coaching should be my career. That was just a joke to myself—I find myself to be hilarious, of course—but that silly thought reminded me of his suggestion that I become a counselor or therapist or whatever. I think he might have been kidding, but the idea actually had sparked interest in me, whereas not much else had before. Despite my various faults, I really do like people and am interested in what makes them tick. And I think all those honesty blasts that freak everyone out are really just me seeing deep inside the heart of things and understanding where the truth lies in messy tangles of emotions. On the other hand, I couldn't exactly be blurting out my every harsh and unfiltered thought to someone who was both needing help and paying me to offer it.

Could I work on those faults, though...?

As I stood under the spray of the shower, I spun that thought around and analyzed it like a 3D model for a while. I'd spent the first twenty-five years of my life shrugging off any hurt I'd caused other people with responses that basically boiled down to *Hey, this is just who I am.* I confess I'd never given much thought to changing myself or trying to be kinder. I should probably buy a "What Would Lily Do" bracelet because, seriously, had I ever actually tried to run my many thoughts and comments and jokes through any kind of quality check first? I don't even know why I asked myself that question, because of course the answer was a big, fat, echoing *no.* Meanwhile, I had a lifetime of evidence strongly suggesting that not everyone thought I was as funny as I did, nor did they necessarily want to hear about the truth as I saw it.

Huh....

My resident rage monkey had given me a lot to think about in his passing comment. But I let all my self-analysis float to the back of my mind as I turned off the shower and reached for my towel. I had to go buy a futon I really didn't need, definitely didn't want, probably had no room for, and certainly couldn't afford.

Yay me.

*   *   *

"Thinking of taking up marathon showering?" Mitch asked when I finally emerged from my room, dressed and ready to go. "I hear there's good money to be made on the European circuit."

"Oh my, we are really funny this morning," I shot back. "Ready to do this? And do you have any idea where we should even start looking?"

"I hear Futons-to-Go has an excellent snack bar," he offered, which made an embarrassingly snorty laugh erupt out of me.

"You're killing me this morning. I wouldn't have taken you for a morning person, but here you are, all loaded up and ready to take me out with your joke arsenal."

"Guess it's my new black-belt-level sleep skills," he said. "Two nights in a row of deep sleep. I'm like a new man."

"Aw, and here I was getting attached to the irritating, grouchy old guy."

"Funny. But seriously, I don't know where to buy a futon. Do they even make them anymore?"

"Ugh, let me look...." I grabbed my phone and did a "futons near me" kind of search. "Get this, there's a store literally called Futon World in Paramus. Oh no, wait, I said 'literally'! Are you gonna get all depressed about losing Tifanee now? Wanna listen to sad songs about girls who use the word 'literally' a lot and then cry a while?"

"Oh no, my prickly friend," he said. "If I don't go to Futon World, I will literally die."

I don't know why we both laughed as hard as we did at his dumb comment, but I was wiping away tears when we finally got our crap together enough to leave the apartment and head down to the parking lot.

"Did you pay extra for the rust?" he asked then, his nose wrinkling in disdain as he warily eyed my car. "Is that why the hubcaps took off? Embarrassed to be associated with this abomination?"

"I'm glad you like it, too!" I said, unlocking the doors. "Also take note of this sweet remote and old-school separate key."

"Neato," he said weakly, which made me laugh again. I don't know when we'd crossed over from jerks to jokes, but I liked it. Probably a little too much.

Nevertheless, our first actual friction of the day came at the store. I kept trying out the smallest, cheapest models I could find, but Mitch, meanwhile, was asking about mattress firmness and stuff like that. I guess those black-belt sleep skills were paying off for him, because he sure had a load of questions for the sales team. Eventually I blurted out my worries right into the middle of his analysis.

"Here's the thing," I began. "I know I offered to split the cost of this with you, but I can't afford that top-of-the-line stuff you keep eyeballing. Come on, you've seen my car. Let's buy the futon without hubcaps, okay?"

"I got shoved into your life, and you essentially had no say in the matter when Lily fluttered her eyes at you," he said. "Also, I've been all inappropriately handsy in my sleep, and you haven't complained once. And yesterday, after my family invaded your personal space, you just rolled with it. Honey badger or not, you've been a great sport. So the least I could do is buy you a piece of furniture."

"Thanks," I said. "And, uh, okay, I guess. I appreciate it, sort of. I appreciate the *gesture*. Not going to lie though: I don't actually *want* a futon. We're going to hurt the Barbie couch's feelings. And where's it going to go, anyway?"

"I know it's not ideal," he went on, "but maybe we can talk Lily into dumping that couch. Or we could shove it in my mom's garage or something. I'm not sure how long I'm going to be here. I can't keep turning you into a human burrito every night. It's weird."

"This whole situation is so weird that the burrito thing is like the normal part," I replied. "But sure, knock yourself out. It has to get delivered, though. Either that or Jake needs to show up with his truck."

And with that, I became the begrudging owner of a monstrosity of a futon. Plus, Mitch got his wish to sleep alone that night. I missed him; I'm not going to start hiding the truth now. I rolled around that night, a million questions and worries tossing through my mind. I still believed it was stupid and futile, but I guess I was developing some kind of a crush on the guy, out of my league or not. So, unfortunately for me, I didn't just miss his warmth; I missed the conversation and laughter, too. Somehow, in two short nights together, he'd rearranged everything I thought I knew about him. I'd told him I wasn't sure I liked him. For once, I hadn't been tossing out a harsh truth grenade; nope, that had been a lie.

I was freezing and lonely as I lay there, but I finally fell asleep. Then, a short time later, I was jerked awake by yelling. It took a second or two for me to realize it was Mitch. I jumped out of bed and raced into the living room, expecting to find him wrestling with an intruder or something.

What I saw instead broke my heart. He was thrashing around on the futon, crying out nonsensical words. I didn't understand any of it, but I did understand that he was in pain.

"Hey, shhh," I whispered, sitting next to him and rubbing gentle circles on his back. "Mitch, you're okay. Do you hear me? You're safe."

"Claire?" he asked, visibly struggling to shake off the chains of confusion.

"Yeah, it's me," I was talking in the soothing tones

people use to calm an upset child. "You were having a nightmare. Man, your sleep sensei would be so mad."

"Stay with me?" he asked, so much vulnerability clear in his sad eyes and hesitant words. "Please?"

"One human burrito, coming up," I said, crawling right into his arms.

Chapter 21

New Feelings, Old Agreement

WELL, THAT had been a complete disaster....

We spent an entire day shopping for a futon she didn't need or want, only for me to find out that my ability to sleep definitely wasn't about that mattress of hers. Once Claire joined me in the living room, I slept *great*. And obviously it wasn't only because I was back home and facing my family, thereby shedding some emotional turmoil. Nope…exercise in futility or not, the futon experiment had answered all my questions—namely, that my newfound peace at night was only about her. *Claire* was the calm in my storm and the answer to my restless, nightly suffering. That wasn't even the shocking part though. No, what had me completely flabbergasted was that she sort of had the same effect on me during our waking hours, too.

Not only did I need her in my arms like a security blanket, I think I was slowly starting to believe that I simply enjoyed being in her presence, no matter where we were or what we were doing. I mean, the sample size was still very small, of course. But I'd laughed harder and more often with her during our futon-a-thon than I had in all my other years combined. It was a lot to wrap my brain around.

Was I *falling* for her? Surely not, right? She certainly wasn't my usual type, although I guess that was a stupid comparison since no previous relationships had come close to cutting through my many layers of angry chaos.

None of those women had calmed me or touched my soul the way Claire had done so effortlessly in such a short amount of time.

What was it about her that appealed to me, though? I was a professional secret-keeper after all, and she was anything *but* closed-off or restrained. She seemed comfortable in letting any old crazy joke or observation thud spectacularly in the middle of any conversation or setting without embarrassment. Nothing bothered her or upset her. She put up with my angry energy and cheerfully dished it right back at me. She wasn't bogged down in self-doubts or angst. She simply was herself, with her snappy comebacks, fierce love for Lily, admitted career uncertainty, and box of Doritos. But hey, the phrase *opposites attract* was commonplace for a reason, right? It packed some truth into its weakly worn-out punch.

Well...great. That was just what this whole situation with my family and my hoard of secrets needed—yet another secret. Because I sure couldn't blurt out how I was feeling to her. For one thing, she didn't even like me, something I didn't have to wonder or guess, thanks to her unrelenting open-book policy. The other factor was that I had no plans to stick around anyway. I had an apartment for at least another year, and I wasn't yet convinced that coming back home was the right move for me in the first place, lease or not. So, regardless of whether it ended up being for one year or longer, Claire and I would soon be on opposite coasts.

That thought sent an ache dragging itself across my chest. Yeah, if I knew nothing else, I knew one thing: I was going to miss her. Plus, all my secrets were eating me up inside. That's what my nightmare had been about. My dreams had dragged me right back to that day my dad had sent Max to the emergency room, and into years of being imprisoned by silence. When Mom and Jake took Max to the hospital, that's when my dad and I had our confrontation.

I flipped out on him as soon as they left; years of pent-up anger came flying through my fists as I launched myself at him. I was just a kid, though, and he quickly had me pinned against the wall. So I started hurling insults and accusations and hate at him instead of fists. And in one of those angry, verbal missiles, I accidentally hit a bullseye and guessed a truth he was ready to destroy me to protect.

There's a lot of pain involved with me offering up even that small amount of detail. I've spent years trying to lock that day deep inside me. But it constantly fought back against my restraints, and it usually won its freedom each night in those restless dreams of mine.

On that day in question, my father and I struck a bargain. I wouldn't tell, but he wouldn't have to send me to the hospital too or risk inevitable jail time in order to silence me. No, all he had to do was leave Max alone. No more comments. No more insults. And please God, no more fists. Nope—no more anything. Pretending Max didn't exist would earn my silence. For my part, I'd leave so I wouldn't be tempted to blurt it all out. That was the deal. I guess "blackmail" wasn't exactly the right word to describe it. It was more like an agreement born out of mutual desperation.

And it had mostly worked. He got rid of me, and I left with his stupid truths in tow. In exchange, he never interacted with Max again, and he did nothing to prevent Jake from removing Max from the house as soon as he could.

Max eventually found his freedom. So did Jake.

Then they met incredible women to love, finally shaking off our terrible childhoods for good. Their futures were bright, and their happiness was secured.

Mine sure wasn't, but hey, we don't always get everything we want. My mind fluttered back to my newly acknowledged feelings for the woman still asleep and wrapped in my arms. No, my story definitely wasn't going to have the same sweet ending that my brothers had found in their lives. But as long as they were both happy, that's all that mattered.

That's all that had *ever* mattered.

Chapter 22

Jokes and Confessions

MITCH STILL LOOKED haunted when I woke up. But since I'm me, I couldn't merely let him stew in his worries, quiet and unremarked upon. Nope, I needed to parade that elephant in the room right past him.

"Hey, so the futon thing worked out great, huh?" I asked, happy that my sarcasm drew up the corners of his mouth as he glanced down at me.

"If you liked that awesome idea, then stick with me, babe," he said, squeezing me more tightly for reasons I decided not to analyze...much. "I'm filled with ideas for plans that end up getting me nowhere so, in reality, you're only seeing the shadowy edges of my incredible powers."

"Nightmares, huh?" I said, swatting away our attempts at silliness now. "That's why you typically can't sleep?"

"Yup. All the memories I spend my waking hours suppressing come bubbling to the surface at night, but that's only if I can actually get to sleep in the first place. Other times I just roll around and overthink everything."

"I'm no therapist, although your suggestion that maybe I could be one has had me thinking. But my point here is that, trained or not, it seems pretty obvious you're never going to have long-term peace until you face those memories head on, honey-badger style."

"You're thinking about being a therapist, huh? I have to say, I love that idea for you. No one cuts through pleasantries and fakeness and gets right to the truth like you do. That totally fits, although you probably won't be able to say half the stuff you're thinking to your patients or clients or whatever they're called."

"Nope, and that's the problem with the plan. But shut up with your attempts to divert my attention. Are you almost ready to spill your secrets to your brothers? Until you do, I think you're going to be restless and haunted at night, while making the whole world think you're a selfish jerk by day."

He shrugged. "Maybe I *am* a selfish jerk, though. Remember all that stuff you said about having negative expectations of me? You think I'm a jerk, too, and we just established you can identify hidden truths."

"I did think that, yeah. But you're kind of growing on me."

"Like mold?"

"Exactly!" I said with a short laugh. "But you're like the cool black mold that's so deadly and insidious that it has to be removed professionally or everyone nearby gets sick."

"All I heard there is that you think I'm cool."

"Right, that's what I said," I replied, happy to get him joking with me again. The haunted vulnerability I'd seen in his eyes in the middle of the night had mostly vanished. "But you're still trying to avoid what I asked. What's stopping you from blasting your secrets all over the place like you've got a super-soaker filled with truth? Max and Jake are begging you to do it, so I can't figure out what's stopping you. I can't imagine why you wouldn't want to do absolutely anything to get rid of those nightmares and find some peace."

He sighed and let go of me, making a big show of flexing and shaking his arms to get the circulation flowing again. It was like he needed to drive home the point of what a heavy lump and burden I was, the jerk.

"Stop flexing like I broke your arms and focus here," I told him.

"Ooh, is someone enjoying the gun show?" he asked, stopping to pump his muscles at me. Ugh, I *was* enjoying the gun show, darn it.

"Okay, I get it," I went on. "You can stop with your stupid jokes. I'm not the right person to open up to, so don't even bother rolling out your 'I'm not family' excuse. I get it. All I'm saying is that you desperately need to open up to *someone*. That's where your sanity lies, I'm afraid."

Once that speech made its confident appearance, I dramatically got up and swung my feet off my side of the futon, which wasn't all that comfortable despite his attempt at ferreting out the perfect one.

"Do you work today?" he asked, a funny look on his face accompanying the sudden question and topic shift.

"Yeah, but not until later this afternoon. Only a few hours though. Honestly, it's barely worth the gas. Not sure what Cynthia was thinking there, but whatever."

"Does that mean you've got some time this morning?"

"Sure, I guess. Wait...I should have asked what you're thinking first. What am I agreeing to here?"

"Do you want to come with me to talk with my family?" He sounded almost nervous to hear my reply. *Huh. What's that about?* I wondered as he drew in a deep breath and continued. "Since it's Saturday, Melody invited us all over for brunch. Might be the perfect time to unload a secret or two."

"Are you serious?!" I shrieked, turning back around to face him again, leaning on my arm for support. "You're going to do it? You're going to tell them everything?"

"Uh, no, probably not *everything*. I think it's too much to unload at once, and I need to wait to make sure the old man really isn't going to wake up. It's…too soon and too much to say all at the same time."

"Okay," I said, touched he made that offer. "But Melody didn't invite me, so it'd be rude for me to show up unannounced. As you pointed out, I'm not part of your family."

"When I explain that I don't think I can do this without you there, I think she'll pull out an extra plate," he replied, his eyes boring into mine now. His unspoken message was clearly heartfelt and urgent, even if I wasn't successfully interpreting it. Honestly, I didn't fully understand what he was trying to communicate with the words he *had* spoken.

"Me?" I asked, not bothering to hide my shock. "You called me a barnacle a couple days ago. Why would you want me there, attaching myself on the side of your family's pain?"

"Claire, I don't understand it myself. I'm sorry about the barnacle thing. I'm sorry about a lot of stuff, truthfully. All I know is that being with you soothes me. I don't think I can do this without you."

"Ahh, yeah, that's classic Claire," I said, leaning immediately into my old joking defense-mechanisms. It was difficult to believe the words he'd just spoken and almost impossible to acknowledge how deeply they touched me. "I get that a lot."

"Well, I'm not joking here. And I'm not trying to manipulate you. It's the truth."

"*Really?*" I asked, my voice weak and crackling with surprise.

"Really." He reached out and covered the hand I was leaning on. "I meant every word. So? What do you say? Are you willing to come? Help a roomie out?"

Lots of potential jokes lined up in my mind, each more anxious to get a smile out of him than the next. But…well, I think I believed him. And if I *did*, then I also believed and understood that what he needed right then wasn't one of my typical responses.

I leaned back so my weight wasn't on that hand anymore and flipped it over, angling myself so I could lace our fingers together.

"Mitch, if you need me there, I'm there."

Chapter 23

The Vault Starts to Open

IN THE END, I couldn't bring myself to confess to anyone how important it was to have Claire in the room when my secrets finally started rolling out. I texted Jake and asked if Melody minded having an extra person tag along, and of course she didn't. I added a weak joke about not wanting to keep Claire and Lily separated, to throw him off the scent. I wasn't ready to explain the strange and shifting dynamics between Claire and me. I couldn't even explain any of that to myself.

When we arrived, I could feel a little panic starting when I realized Liam was there. I mean, duh, it was *his* home. But still, it was a huge miscalculation. I'd worked myself up into finally being willing to talk, then realized my timing was bad.

"M-Mitch, what's wrong?" Max asked, zeroing in on my obvious discomfort.

"Oh, I just…I had started thinking this morning that maybe today would be a good time to start…uh, shedding a few secrets," I replied, my eyes nervously darting over to where Liam sat with a game controller in his hands. "But this is Melody's party and her home, so I think I'm being selfish trying to take it over. And stupid because I forgot about, uh…little ears."

Jake's eyes shot over to Melody's, and they had some sort of silent conversation that ended in her quickly putting my fears to rest.

"Mitch, when Liam gets screen time, an entire

parade could march through here and he wouldn't notice. So why don't you guys all come sit around the table and talk while I finish up in here? He's fine right there in the living room, and you can say whatever you need to say. Really."

I guess they were even more ready to hear my secrets than I realized, because that comment prompted a scramble for seating that looked like a lightning round of musical chairs. I would have laughed under normal circumstances, but of course that situation was anything but normal or funny. Plus, when the dust cleared, it was obvious there wasn't going to be room for Claire. Not if we left a seat for Melody.

"Oh, uh, I'll just see what Liam's playing, huh?" Claire offered, which spiked more panic in me. Had she already forgotten what she promised?

"Oh no you don't!" Melody said, making me want to send her a long-winded thank you note first thing tomorrow. "Hang on, I've got another chair in the office."

She settled Claire directly across the table from me, and next to Lily, of course. I would have preferred to have her fingers laced with mine again, but that probably wasn't the path to keeping everyone— including Claire—in the dark about my feelings.

All the members of my family were staring at me expectantly, and the looks on their faces and the odd quiet in the room told me they were afraid to do anything that might make me change my mind. I felt bad they thought it was necessary to manage me to that degree, but...well, I suppose they weren't wrong. Part of me *did* want to run for the door.

"Uh, okay, here's the thing," I said, starting off fairly quivery. "Part of what's stopped me from talking is that I don't know how much Max remembers about the day our, uh, family imploded. Do you…?"

I trailed off, scared that I'd be dumping information on my little brother he wasn't ready to handle. But then Claire's eyes met mine, and she gave me an imperceptibly small nod of her head. Her small show of support actually helped me keep going.

"Do you remember the day you stopped talking, Max?" I prompted softly.

He looked a little puzzled, and his glance darted from my face over to Jake's and back again.

"Dad was y-yelling at me, right?" Lily reached over to take one of his hands in hers. She knew what was coming. I'd told her about this the day she showed up at my apartment looking for him but finding me instead.

"Yeah, but he did more than yell that day," Jake added. "A lot more."

Max looked down for a moment and studied the sight of his and Lily's hands together as he thought about it. That moment represented a lot of what I'd been afraid of—that I was reminding him of something he'd successfully buried.

"He p-punched me, didn't he?" Max finally said. Tears fell down Lily's face. Melody, Jake, and Claire all looked like they were fighting them back, too.

"Yeah, he did," I replied. "Jake and Mom took you to the hospital. Do you remember that?"

"N-not really."

"That's because he knocked you out," Jake said. "You had a concussion. Mom lied to the doctor and said you got hit with a baseball. You were fading in and out, and I didn't correct her. I've always regretted that—I'm really sorry, Max. The cops surely would have gotten involved if I'd had the courage to speak up."

"I w-wouldn't have wanted to be s-separated from you," Max said, talking to Jake of course. I'd never be as close to either of them as they were to each other, thanks in large part to what happened that day. "And you w-were just a k-kid, too. None of it w-was your f-fault."

"I did the wrong thing, though," Jake said. "It still haunts me."

"That day haunts me, too," I said after silence fell again. I looked up to meet Claire's eyes, and she gave me another little nod. "After you guys left, I, uh, I flipped out on the old man. I started punching him and kicking him and screaming at him. But, well, I was just a kid, too, and he had me pinned up against the wall pretty quickly."

Someone gasped, but I didn't look up to see who it was. At this point, I had to keep going regardless.

"So I started telling him how much I hated him, and I was yelling all kinds of accusations and…well, just trust me here, I didn't leave anything unsaid."

"I get why you didn't tell Max this before," Jake said, "but I can't believe this is the first time *I'm* hearing any of it. Why didn't you tell me? I don't know why I feel I have to keep repeating this to you, but maybe you actually forgot along the way: We're *twins*. You should have felt like you could tell me anything. You *still* should."

"I wanted to, I swear. But, well, he and I sort of ended up making a deal that day. I've thought of it as blackmail in the past, but I guess that's not the right word. He wanted me gone, really badly. And I just wanted him to stop hurting Max. Well, and to leave

Jake alone, too. So, we…well, I guess we reached a meeting of the minds. If I left and never came back, he'd never touch either of you or belittle Max or even talk to him again. But looking back now, I guess it was too late, wasn't it? The damage had already been done. After that, Max never talked to anyone other than Jake for years."

The silent stares that met me when I looked back up were loaded with astonishment. No one said anything until Max finally found the words to form his reply.

"You d-did this for *m-me?*" he asked, tears starting to slip from his eyes. "I knew J-Jake g-gave up his l-life for me, b-but I never g-guessed *both* my b-brothers did."

"I'd do anything for you Max," I told him. "For both of you. I'm so sorry I haven't been in your lives since that day. It's ripped me apart to the point that I can barely sleep at night or form any other human connections. I missed you both so much, and I never wanted to be isolated and alone like that. Jake, *of course* I didn't forget we're twins. I never wanted to let you down or make you shoulder everything the way you did, but because of me and the choices I made, that's exactly what ended up happening. And then I found out it almost killed you! I was trying to save you both, so I stubbornly stuck to the terms of our deal. I…stayed gone. And now I can't even tell if I did the right thing anymore. I don't know if the decisions I made helped or, in the end, if I just made everything worse for everyone."

"Better," Jake finally said, breaking the silence that once again greeted my words. "We all made choices we regret, I'm sure. But having you back here now has made everything a whole lot better."

Despite my persistent worries and regrets—and the fact that I still had more secrets inside me—I knew he was right. Being together again *was* better.

Chapter 24

Car Conversation Fail

THE REST OF Melody's party quickly got a whole lot happier. I think the fact that Mitch had finally taken a step toward uncorking all his secrets had stuck a pin in the balloon of resentments that slowly had been expanding in his brothers' chests—especially Jake's. They all looked lighter and younger somehow. It was great to witness, not gonna lie. Especially since it was making my girl Lily so happy to see *them* so happy. Many degrees of happiness going on around that table.

But I knew Mitch wasn't done unloading on his brothers, and I could see occasional shades of panic and indecision in his eyes. I think the twin connection was going strong, despite their years apart, because I noticed Jake sneaking a few worried glances at him. They were all relieved, it was true, but there was also a crackle of electricity in the air, like that feeling of pent-up energy right before a storm hits. Jake felt it and didn't like it, that much was clear.

I guess I was buoyed by all the contact joy, right along with the happy—if a little confusing—feelings that Mitch had unleashed when he asked me to go to the party with him. It came bubbling out when I pushed him about the rest of what he was hiding as soon as we got in the car to go home...er, back to *my* apartment, where he was currently holding the position of resident squatter.

"When are you going to tell them the rest of it?" I demanded, as blunt as ever.

"What makes you think there's more?" he asked as if he hadn't told me that very morning that he wasn't ready to spill *all* his truths yet.

"*You* made me think it, dummy," I replied. "This morning on the futon you said you wanted to start spilling your secrets, but you didn't think it was time yet to dump them all. When do you think it'll be time?"

"I told you, I need to see what happens with my dad's health, first. And don't start pushing me about this."

"It's pretty obvious what the secret has to do with," I said, ignoring his testy tone. "You sure glossed over the part about *why* your dad was so hopped up on goofballs to push you out of their lives. You know something he didn't want anyone else to know, don't you?"

"So, just to be clear, this is you *not* pushing me?" he asked, fire in his eyes now. "What does you being pushy look like? Wait, no, don't answer that. I don't want to know."

"Hey, dude, you're the one who pointed out that I'm good at seeing to the heart of things. Don't act all surprised when I show off my mad skills."

"Wow, you're so deep and intuitive," he said, fully furious now. I spared a glance over at him just to admire the sight. Mad Mitch was a different level of hot than normal Mitch. I was astonished that it was even possible for him to level up, but there we were. "Of *course* I knew things he didn't want me telling anyone else. Like maybe the fact that he'd just sent his young son to the hospital? I threatened to call the cops, and he threatened to kill me. Boom, there you have it. That's how we came around to agreeing on a different path and set of outcomes."

"So that's your other secret?" I asked, not at all convinced. "You're saying that your psyche is eating you from the inside out every night because you've been hiding that he threatened to kill you?"

"I said what I said," he replied, as though that argument would hold up in court.

"Riiight," I said. "Have it your way. Don't tell me. I just thought we'd taken a step forward this morning and reached a level of trust or—dare I say it?—friendship. But, hey, I can see I was wrong."

"We're hostile roommates at best," he said, really digging in now.

Guess I really did touch a nerve—but that didn't stop me, either. I don't know why I was being so relentless with him, but the haunted look in his eyes from that morning was kind of taking a turn at haunting *me*. I think I wanted to do whatever it took to push him into setting himself free. If I had to offer myself up as tribute to feed the rage machine, so be it.

"Sure we are," I said. "Hostile roommates who cuddle like teenage newlyweds every night and tell secrets in the dark."

"Claire!" he shouted in decibels extremely unnecessary inside a Corolla. "Leave me alone! Do you hear me? *Leave...me...alone!* We're not friends. We're not cuddle bunnies. We're nothing, okay? Nothing. And people who are nothing to each other don't share their deepest, darkest secrets."

"So you admit you still have deep, dark secrets?" I hammered on, utterly unable to help myself. Plus, yeah, I sort of felt like lashing out at the big doofus. I know he was just in pain, but I wasn't his punching bag, nor would I ever sign up for that job. Struggling or not, jerks gonna jerk.

"I'm going to the gym with my brothers," he said, acting like I hadn't said anything. Nice. "Have fun at work."

"Great," I replied. "Be sure to take out all that man rage on something not named Claire, mm-kay?"

Stony silence was his only reply, and when we got back to the apartment, he couldn't change into his gym clothes and get out of there fast enough. He went out of his way to not even look at me or say goodbye.

So, yeah—that went well.

Chapter 25

The Apology

I THOUGHT finally releasing some of my secrets would make me feel happy and maybe even relieved. But the energy inside me sure didn't feel like either of those emotions.

I was stressed out because I knew we needed to stage that whole emotional scene again—and my brothers' reactions might not be fueled by so much love and gratitude and understanding the next time. Nope, the rest of my hidden truths were barbed and dangerous. They'd been punching holes inside me for years, so I knew how accurate that description was. They were sure to hit my brothers with the same jagged intensity, and that's what had me so amped up.

That's also why I'd taken my anger out on Claire in the car, who definitely hadn't deserved any of it. I know she simply had been trying to help. And she was so right that she *should* have felt able to broach tough and sensitive subjects with me. We definitely had taken steps toward being closer; she hadn't read that wrong. She'd suggested we might even be friends.

Yeah....

It was true—we somehow had moved toward something that felt like friendship. But it also felt like more than that. We'd started as basically enemies, and I honestly don't understand how or why the relationship morphed so quickly. One minute we were at each other's throats, the next we were laughing in her bed and snuggling together in our sleep. Yeah, we were definitely friends now, and we were obviously something more, too. Really, how could I have even tried to deny it to her? Not after how desperately I'd needed her strong presence with me at the table that morning.

But thanks to me and my inability to control my rage, she surely wanted us to march right back to the beginning and straight into our enemies stage again. I didn't want that, though. I *really* didn't want that. I owed her an apology. I owed her a *river* of apologies.

"Hey Jake!" someone said at the gym. I looked around before realizing they were talking to me. I simply waved in return, not in the mood for conversation. I showed my visitor's pass at the front desk and was met with another confused look. I'd forgotten how strange being a twin can be.

Jake's gym didn't have a punching bag, which is something I desperately missed. I settled on some machines instead, deciding to make it a leg day. Even though working the bag is a better stress reliever, I was feeling somewhat calmer when Jake walked up.

"I had someone tell me they thought I was wearing a different outfit today," he said, "so I figured I'd find you here."

"Yeah, sorry," I replied, not feeling sorry at all. "Someone said hi to you, and I didn't bother to correct him."

"You know I work here, right?"

"Sorry, man. Got a lot on my mind."

"I know you do. And I'm proud of you, you know. Proud that you finally told us. Proud to learn that you were looking out for us. Proud that you willingly walked the lonely road you chose to try to save Max."

"Yeah, well, I'm proud of *you* for staying and actually helping him survive," I said, shrugging off his praise. I wasn't sure there was much about me worth being proud of, honestly.

He studied me for a moment. "Something else on your mind? When you left Melody's, I thought maybe you'd turned a corner. But here you are, looking all ragey again."

"I took my anger out on Claire," I told him. "I said some stuff to her that I didn't mean and that she definitely didn't deserve. So now I'm here feeling guilty."

"Something going on with you two? You're always at each other's throats, but maybe that's just chemistry?"

"Not sure," I said, not thrilled at the thought of dumping out my confusing thoughts and emotions where Claire was concerned. On the other hand, not talking to anyone ever about anything is what landed me in this situation—the one in which I couldn't communicate without getting angry. "There's a lot I like about her. She's strong and hilarious and always, *always* honest. I've never known anyone like her."

"I wasn't totally sure about her at first," he replied, and I could feel irritation rising inside me. I hoped he wasn't about to tear her down. "But the bond she and Lily have is so strong. I think under all those sarcastic comments and defense mechanisms is a heart every bit as golden as Lily's or Melody's. She's just better at hiding it behind all the sass."

I chuckled. "She's sassy alright. Part of me wants to spar with her, and part of me wants to grab her and never let go."

"So grab her and never let go *while* sparring," he

said, as though that comment made sense. "What's stopping you?"

"Jake, I'm not staying here long term. I told you: I have a lease on my apartment."

"So stay here with us rent-free and just ride it out. Or go back for a year and then move here permanently. Come on man, your isolation is over. The deal with Dad is null and void now. He sure isn't in any position to enforce it. You're miserable; anyone can see that. Stop making excuses and start laying down tracks toward making a life here. Then you can date Claire and see what happens."

"I can't casually date Lily's best friend," I said, actively fighting off how easy he made it all sound. "What happens when we inevitably destroy each other? It's going to make everything awkward."

"But what happens if you *don't* destroy each other? What if the sparks we all see between the two of you are the start of something huge? Maybe someone as fierce and feisty as Claire is precisely what a grouchy loner like you needs."

"We'll see what happens," I offered lamely.

Then I successfully changed the topic by raving about Melody's cooking.

*   *   *

Jake's words stuck with me, though, as did my remorse over the way I'd treated Claire. I knew I needed to show up with more than just apologies. So when she walked in the door that night, I was ready.

"Hey, I messed up," I began the moment the door clicked shut behind her. "I was a moody jerk this morning, and you didn't deserve any of it. And you were right: We *are* friends and cuddle bunnies. So here, please take this gift as a sign of exactly how sorry I am."

Her face simultaneously displayed puzzlement and amusement—she was amuzzled—as she stared at my peace offering.

"You bought me a bag of Doritos?"

"Yeah. But did you notice it's the party-size bag, though? That's got to count for something."

She nodded. "I did notice that."

"Want to sit and watch some TV together while we eat them?" I asked, surprised by exactly how much I wanted her to say yes.

"Okay. And I accept your apology and your gift. But if you try to eat any of them, the arm you draw back won't have a hand attached to it anymore."

I laughed, and she gave me a smile. Her forgiveness felt like a priceless treasure, and as much as I didn't want to think too hard about it, I grabbed up that feeling and held onto it.

Chapter 26

The Text

WE DIDN'T EVEN bother pretending that Mitch sleeping on the futon was an option that night. I mean, as much as I hadn't really wanted it, I have to admit it had been the perfect spot for us to stretch out and chill while we watched television together. It was also a great place to be while we were enjoying the truce we'd reached. But when it was bedtime, he just looked at me, and I nodded my head. I knew exactly what he was probably afraid to ask, but he didn't need to worry. I would have done just about anything to help him have trauma-free sleep.

It mostly worked, too. We crawled into bed and both of us fell asleep pretty quickly on our opposite sides. But I suppose neither of us was all that surprised the next morning to find that at some point in the night, we'd wrapped ourselves together again. Awake, we could be a boiling pot of fiery tension. But our subconscious minds clearly didn't care about any of that. In sleep, we simply enjoyed the comforts offered by our time together. I didn't understand it any more than Mitch likely did, but when I snuggled deeper into his arms that morning, he simply tightened his hold on me.

"You working today?" he asked, his voice a sexy morning growl.

"Yeah. I start early with the lunch crowd."

"I should contact my agent and see if she's got

anything lined up for me," he said. "I can't lay around not making any money forever."

I was about to make some quip about that—I don't remember which direction my mind was headed with what surely would have been a hilarious comment—when his phone buzzed.

"Huh, thought I turned it off," he mumbled, pulling away to reach for it. He rolled on his back and read the text, a look of pain suddenly shadowing his features.

"What's wrong?" I asked.

"Uh, well, it's Jake," he said, rubbing his hand over his face, which was darkened with morning scruff. He looked deliciously rumpled, but so sad, too. "Hospital called him to say we're nearing the end. Dad's organs are starting to shut down. Time for final goodbyes or whatever."

"Uh…you look confused—are you feeling conflicted about whether that's good news or bad?" I asked, utterly uncertain what to say because he looked so lost. "I know you guys have a whole tractor trailer filled with dad issues, anger, and regrets. Seems like confusion is about the right response here."

"You're not wrong about that," he replied. "In a way, yeah, we should start planning a party, not a funeral. But...."

"But part of you still loves him simply because he's your dad?" I guessed, my words whispered and cautious.

"Is that crazy?" he asked, turning to look at me now. "I *hated* that man. He ruined our lives. But, well, I guess a part of me still remembers the dad he was to Jake and me when we were kids. That dad was a good man. He did silly stuff like let us ride on his back through the living room, and he helped us build ridiculously complicated forts in the backyard. I miss that man, and I wish he'd never left."

"Nothing you just said is crazy, and neither is anything you're feeling," I told him. "My dad had a heart attack at his desk at work and died before his coworkers even noticed. I was twelve at the time, and I spent years being mad at him about it. Part of me is still sort of angry that he left with no warning and no goodbyes. I know that doesn't make any sense, but human emotions are complicated."

"I'm sorry he left you," Mitch said. "You still have your mom?"

"Yeah, remember? I told you I could go stay with her and give you the apartment? She still lives in the house I grew up in, and I think part of her is secretly hoping it was all a mix-up and he'll come walking through the door any time now."

"That's so sad," he said. "Siblings?"

"Yeah," I said. "I've got a brother, Chad, who Lily used to be obsessed with, big time. Like, for years. Little hearts around his name in her notebooks and the whole works. If you ever want to get Max's blood pressure jumping, make comments about bringing Chad around more."

"Okay, thanks for the info," he said with a laugh. "Are you two close?"

"Uh, we are, and we aren't, I guess. I don't talk to him, not like this. But we joke around a lot. And we'd have each other's backs if everything hit the ceiling."

"That's good," he said, staring at said ceiling now.

"So what's the plan? You need to get up and head over to the hospital?"

Mitch gave a weight-of-the-world kind of slow

exhale. "Yeah, but first we're going to go to my mom's house. See if she wants to say goodbye. It's not going to be easy. Max and me, we, uh…well, neither of us has been there in years, and we never planned to return, you know?"

"I know," I said. "Complicated emotions and stuff. I get it."

"Yeah," he said, suddenly swinging his gaze back to me. "I just realized I don't even know your last name."

For some reason, the urgent tone combined with the major topic shift struck me as funny, so I laughed hard a while as Mitch studied me with an amused look on his face.

"What was that about?" he asked.

"It just seemed so silly," I said. "Here we are, all up in each other's psyches, but you don't even know my name. It's…weird I guess."

"I think you could argue that lots of stuff to do with us is weird," he replied. "So? What, you don't have a last name?"

"Oh, yeah, I do," I said. "It's Chambers, actually."

"Your brother's name is Chad Chambers?"

This set me off laughing again, and this time I had no idea why. Simple release of emotions and tension, I guess.

"You're such a nut," he finally said, leaning over to plant a kiss on my forehead before swinging his legs off the bed.

"Did you just forehead kiss me like I'm three?" I asked.

"Yes?" he said, looking back over his shoulder at me. "You were giving off major toddler energy there, so it tracks."

"Okay, well...do you need me to go with you today?" I asked, studying his eyes for hints as to what he was thinking.

"I know you've got to work," he said finally. "And yes, part of me is dying to bring you with me. I don't understand it, Claire Chambers, not one bit. But for some reason, being with you makes me feel better. It seems to make *everything* better. But I'll be with my brothers, so I guess I'll be okay."

I smiled at him as he gave me one last look, then he stood and headed for the bathroom.

I'd never been told that being with me made everything better. Not by anyone. How had a closed-off anger generator just given me the best compliment of my life?

And why was I increasingly unable to imagine standing back silently and waving goodbye as he flew back to his life in California without me?

Chapter 27

The Final Goodbye

I WASN'T READY to face my mom, and I didn't realize *how* not ready I was until the three of us walked into the house and saw just how disoriented she'd become.

"Jake, you brought along visitors!" she said, flushing as she nervously patted her hair. It used to be a beautiful deep mahogany color, but now it was mostly gray and currently flattened to the back of her head thanks to a particularly bad case of pillow sculpting. "Hello, boys!"

"Mom, you know it's Mitch and Max, right?" Jake asked, looking at the two of us with a wild, questioning eyeroll. "You're always asking if I brought my brothers with me. Well, guess what? I finally did."

"That's nice, dear," she said, looking at us both with confusion shining in her eyes. "Oh, yes, I see it now. Hello, Mitchell. But...Colin? What are you doing here?"

"Colin?" Jake asked. "Mom, come on, who are you talking about? There's no Colin."

"M-Mom, it's me," Max cut in, a sliver of hurt audible in his words. "It's *M-Max.*"

"Oh, yes, of course, honey," she said. "Come here! Let me hug you both. It's been so long!"

"Hey Jake," I whispered as our mother fussed with getting Max settled onto the couch in a nest of throw pillows following an awkward round of hugs. "Is this senility, day drinking, or a psychotic break?"

"I'm thinking it's drinking combined with the systematic avoidance of reality," he replied. "I've tried a million times to get her to go to the doctor, but forget it. Since dad's accident, she rarely leaves the house anymore."

"It's brutal," I said. "I had no idea she was this far gone."

"Neither did I, and I'm here almost daily. I think having you guys here is throwing her."

"What are you two whispering about?" she asked. "That's always the way it was with you two, wasn't it? I'd always heard about the twin connection, but my goodness. I had no idea how real it was until you teamed up against the rest of us. Your father always thought it was something else and just another sign of how smart his boys were. He was always so proud of you two!"

Of course I looked over at Max, and of course that comment had landed with a thud and affected him. *Thanks for yet another reminder, Mom.* Yes, our father had been proud of Jake and me. Not Max. Never Max. Well, at least not once the stutter emerged.

"Mom, dad's dying," Jake said, not bothering to soften the message. "We're headed over to the hospital now to say goodbye. Why don't you come with us?"

"Oh no, you boys go on," she said. "I'm not even dressed, and I haven't done my hair."

"Mom, this is *it,*" I said. "This is your last chance to say goodbye to your husband. You stuck with this man through a lot of years and a lot of bad times. *Now* is when you're giving up? Not when he was abusing your sons? That doesn't even make sense."

For a minute it seemed like she'd heard me. Not the odd and disoriented person sitting in Dad's old recliner, but rather the mother I remembered from my childhood. She opened her mouth as though she were going to reply, but in the end, she simply shook her head.

"No, you boys go on," she said. "I'll be just fine here."

"Okay, well, guess that's it," Jake said. "See you tomorrow, Mom."

*   *   *

When we got outside, I pulled Max into a hug.

"I'm sorry, bro," I said. "That sucked. The whole thing sucked."

"At least she r-remembered you," Max replied with a shake of his head. "D-don't worry about m-me, though. I stopped c-caring a long t-time ago."

"Yeah, I suppose you had to."

"I d-did."

"Let's get this over with," Jake said, leading us to his truck, where we were all cramming together in the front seat.

"You gonna get rid of this thing now that you've got a kid?" I asked as he drove us to the hospital. "Pickups aren't exactly family friendly."

"Not sure I can let go of it. Although I'm guessing we'll have to get something bigger, too."

"What's with everyone and their relic cars?" I asked. "Have you guys seen that deathtrap Claire drives? Gotta get her into something safer, or I'll have a heart attack thinking about it."

Jake raised an eyebrow at me, and Max swung a surprised look in my direction.

"Are you interested in C-Claire?" Max asked.

"Oh, no…well, I don't know, to be honest," I said. "I do know she's pretty special, though. Smart, funny, incredibly strong…never known anyone like her before."

"She's a g-great person," Max said, "for what it's w-worth. L-Lily adores her, and she's always b-been kind to me."

Silence fell between us then, but Claire stayed on my mind; although, to be honest, she hadn't left it in the first place. I kept remembering how cute she'd looked that morning during her laugh attacks. Can't imagine that anyone else on the planet would have been able to take my mind off all this family drama the way she had. There might not be anything long term between us, but I knew I'd never find anyone quite like her again.

That thought made me much sadder than I'd been before, which surprised me, given what we were about to do.

*   *   *

When we got to our dad's room, we were met with a lot of solemn faces and a whole team of people telling us what was happening. Honestly, I couldn't comprehend much of it. We wanted to donate absolutely anything of his that could be used by another patient, like corneas or whatever, but they said it wouldn't be possible in his case. That sounded about right—that donation largely would have become his greatest contribution to the human race, but he didn't even get that right. It was a realization I didn't want to devote too much mental space to.

Then they were gone, and it was just the three of us staring down at him. This was it; it was time to say goodbye. But I realized as I stood there that I'd said goodbye to him years ago, so this moment suddenly felt like nothing more than a formality.

"Either of you need to say anything?" Jake asked.

"I'm sorry his life turned out the way it did," I began. "I'm sorry he hurt Mom and the three of us. But, well, I guess I feel like we already lost him a long time ago. So I'm not sure what I feel right now is grief."

Jake nodded, and we watched him a few long, quiet moments more before Max broke the silence.

"I f-forgive you," Max said, causing both Jake and me to look at him in amazement. He just shrugged, and it was clear that he wasn't lying to himself or to us. He *really* forgave him. "What? W-with as much l-love as I have inside me for L-Lily and *from* L-Lily, I guess there's n-not much room for h-hate anymore."

That was probably the most beautiful thing any of us could have said in that room, and it was way more than our father deserved.

I whispered goodbye to him, and that was that. When we left, my mind was back on Claire again. And I couldn't help wondering if loving her could push all of the hate from inside of me, too.

Chapter 28

New Claire

WHEN MITCH LEFT with his brothers to go deal with all his terrible family issues, I tried to get up and get motivated. Really, I did.

Well, sort of....

My original plan was to execute a lightning-fast cleaning blitz before it was time to shower and get ready for work. As highly motivated as I was to clean, though—that's some top-notch sarcasm, by the way, and it didn't take much to distract me—my mind wanted instead to float a while on a poofy cloud made from all the soft, fluffy feelings Mitch had stirred up inside me with his compliment. He liked being with me! I made everything better for him simply by being there. *Me.* The very same woman who Sebastian had recently broken up with over my…let's call them communication issues. That woman was the same woman who Mitch enjoyed spending time with.

Aren't self-esteem struggles a fun guest and festive addition to any mental party? Because it was a whole lot easier to believe that Sebastian was right in thinking I had no tact, and therefore wasn't a good partner, than it was to believe Mitch found high value in spending time in my company. And no, Mitch hadn't simply been polite. That wasn't the relationship we'd established with each other at all. For as much as I said anything that popped into my mind, Mitch was a bit of a truth bomber himself, at least with me. We were kind of similar in that way. Maybe that was the attraction—we saw ourselves in each other.

That thought made me snort out a disbelieving laugh. Ha! Me? The same as freaking *Mitch,* who looked like he'd been handcrafted by the gods as a thank-you gift to humanity? *As if.* Honestly, that very topic was what prevented me from diving headlong into a full-blown, hearts-in-my-eyes, mega crush on him. We had so much fun together, and we understood each other on a cellular level. Or at least that's how it seemed sometimes. Both of those things were absolutely true. But solid tens don't date sixes or sevens, or whatever I am. Well, okay, with enough effort I could bump to eight, especially in low lighting. *Ugh, whatever....* The point is that he and I weren't the same on the outside. I spent a moment resenting his stupid beautiful face and his irritatingly drool-inducing six pack. Why'd I have to start getting sloppy feelings for someone so far out of my reach?

Okay, so yeah—I knew he'd never be mine to keep forever. Just keeping it real here. But I'd always be grateful for the short time we'd had together. He'd made me feel accepted and valued. Plus he was the one who had me thinking about a specific career path after years of frustration and fuzzy indecision. For that alone, I'd always remember him fondly.

At that thought, I reached over, grabbed my phone, and started doing a little research. What would be involved with this career path I'd started thinking about thanks to him? What sort of training and schooling were we talking about here? What's the difference between a counselor and a therapist and a psychologist? I had a million questions, but my research helped me sort through some of them. Mostly what I learned was that my bachelor's degree was a nice starting point, but I'd need at least a master's, and then I'd have even more decisions to make about which path to take next. But I could do that, right? I could keep slogging through my day job while starting to take some classes. Maybe I could even find an online program to make the experience easier to fit into my life.

I started researching some of the local universities before realizing it was time to get up and get moving. Looked like that cleaning blitz wouldn't be happening.

I'm pretending here that it ever had a chance.

*   *   *

I got through a long shift that only partially served as a distraction from all the questions, plans, and thoughts running around the track in my brain. And despite how excited I was to start applying to master's programs, thoughts about Mitch seemed to keep winning each of the races. It wasn't even close.

When I got home and closed the door, I found Mitch sitting on the futon, alone and in the dark. Alarmed, I flipped on the light to get a better look.

"Hey," I said. "Mitch? You're kind of worrying me here. Are you okay?"

He shook his head, sighed, and then stood up. We just stood there a moment, looking at each other. I had no idea what was going on. No, wait...I take that back. Of *course* I knew what was going on. He'd just been through an emotional wringer of a day, and I didn't know what to do about it. My usual go-to plan was to drop a joke into the middle of any situation, appropriate or not. Or to just come straight out and ask exactly how hard the day had sucked.

But I guess this was a whole new Claire—the one who made everything better and who was starting to roll out some plans to become a therapist. *This* Claire swallowed all potential jokes and comments and questions. And then I simply opened up my arms and started walking toward him. My action seemed to light a flame inside him, because he moved forward, too.

Then he was in my arms.

Chapter 29

Futon Therapy Session

"I'M SO SORRY you're going through this," she said, pulling out of our hug to look at me. "What can I do to help? You told me this morning that I make things better for you. But I guess I don't know exactly what you meant by that. And I definitely don't know what you *need* right now."

"You don't have to do or say anything," I told her, utter honesty loaded into each word. "That hug alone made me feel like maybe I can get through this."

She gave me a shy-looking half smile, which was a total mismatch with the bold and confident woman she typically presented to the world. Maybe I was rearranging her insides in the same way she was restacking mine. I thought all of this as I watched the cute hesitation dance across her face.

"Wanna hang out on the futon?" she asked. "You could tell me about your crappy day. Or not. Totally up to you."

"One futon therapy session coming up," I said, reaching for her hand as we moved over to said futon, which was still awkwardly jammed in front of the couch and basically eating up the entire room.

The living-room-eating-futon situation wouldn't have been such a problem if we just folded it into its sleek sofa formation and stopped pretending that I'd ever sleep on it again. We could have done that, sure, but it was way too comfortable when we watched television—or held impromptu therapy sessions, apparently. Abandoning the futon right where it currently stood hadn't been something we'd really discussed, but we seemed to agree on it since the two of us had been carefully shuffling around it without complaining. I guess we'd have to keep right on shuffling, and acting like the whole thing hadn't been a ridiculous waste of money, at least while I was staying here. Maybe helping Lily stash her couch somewhere could be my parting gift to Claire before I flew back to California.

As soon as that thought popped into my head, I was instantly sorry for allowing it to form. It hurt to think about leaving, but it also hurt to think about staying. Everything hurt and nothing made sense. I felt lost, adrift in a rising tide of conflicting emotions and regrets.

I guess I wasn't doing a particularly good job of hiding any of this because, although we'd flopped down with some normal, we're-just-friends space between us, Claire was suddenly leaning up on one elbow trying hard to take a visual inventory of my many messy emotions.

"Stop worrying about me," I said, opening my arms to her the way she'd done for me when she got home. "C'mere. Let's pretend it's already morning."

She smiled and snuggled into my arms, her head on my shoulder and her hair tickling my face.

"Today sucked, basically," I said. "All of it. My mom's mind seems to be slipping away, or at least her desire to care about anything is disappearing. She didn't even recognize Max, and she had zero interest in saying goodbye to her husband of…I don't even know. Twenty years? Thirty? She stood right by his side during the times when he was abusing Max, and then when he drove all three of us away. She even lied to the doctors about the day his abuse became physical. But *now* she turns on him? Now, when it can't help any of us? I thought my dad was the clear winner in the race to see which one of them could let us down the most, but I'm starting to think her second-place finish was way closer than I ever realized."

"Oh, Mitch, I'm so sorry," Claire said. "I can't imagine how you and your brothers even waded out of that gene pool. Your parents didn't deserve any of you, because you guys are awesome."

"Max and Jake are, anyway," I replied, quickly dismissing her compliment. "Max, despite the kick in the teeth he'd gotten earlier when Mom didn't recognize him, even went to the hospital and proceeded to offer *forgiveness* to the old man. Can you believe that? After everything Dad did to him, Max stood right there and said that Lily had filled him up with so much love that he no longer had room for hate."

"Wow. I...I can't even imagine that. But I'm so happy for Max. Well, and for Lily, too, of course. That's the dream, isn't it? Finding someone who loves you so hard that it pushes away the bad stuff? I can't even imagine me finding someone like that. The sheer enormity of how hard they'd have to love me to fix my bad stuff is mind boggling."

I leaned down to drop a kiss on her head. "Oh, I don't know. Loving you doesn't sound like such a chore to me."

The minute the words came out of my mouth, I could feel her stiffen up. And that made me want to start backtracking and over-explaining what I meant, which surely would have made the moment even more awkward. I didn't mean to lead her on, after all. Since I had no idea how I felt about almost anything in my life, I definitely shouldn't be throwing around a word like "love" with all its shades and colors and not-so-hidden implications.

In the end, though, I decided that I *did* mean what I'd said. Any man lucky enough to love and be loved by Claire surely wouldn't find it difficult at all.

"Anyway," I went on, "we said our goodbyes, and Jake dropped us off here. But then he went back and sat at the old man's bedside for the rest of the afternoon, just so he wouldn't be alone when he died."

"Oh…uh, wow, okay," she said, sort of stumbling over her words. "He didn't ask you two to hang back and sit with him?"

"We didn't know that's what he was planning. He told us about it later. Said he didn't want to put that burden on either of us. Sent us a text to let us know when it finally happened, though. Melody was also in the room when he died, I guess. But no, Jake didn't ask us to be there, and honestly it never occurred to me to offer. Jake said Max already paid his dues in suffering, and I paid mine in my exile. He said it was his turn, as if he really had a debt to pay. As though he didn't give up his teens and most of his twenties to caring for everyone except himself."

"I'm so glad Melody was there for him," Claire said. "I'm sure she was filling him up with love and pushing out all the bad stuff for him, just like Lily did with Max. He'll be okay, Mitch. You all will. The three of you have proven over and over that you're strong enough to survive anything. Nothing that happened today changes any of that."

"I guess. Doesn't it make me a bad person for not

really being sad about his actual death, though? Isn't that sort of messed up?"

"Human emotions are complicated and messy. Of course your feelings about him are confusing, and some of them are awful. But that doesn't make you a bad person. Give yourself time to process it. I'd be willing to bet there's some grief and sadness hiding in the middle of all those other emotions."

I actually smiled then. "You're going to make an incredible therapist. I meant what I said this morning—you make everything better."

"Classic Claire strikes again!" she announced. "But remember: You're awesome, too. I don't want to hear you talking like you're not every bit as amazing and strong and wonderful as your brothers. You *are*, Mitch. Not as awesome as *me*, of course. But you're getting there."

And there she was—my funny, confident Claire was back.

I needed to think more about the things she'd said and about my feelings regarding my dad's death. And also about why I'd just thought of her as "my Claire."

We sat quietly in a warm embrace as her words and my many emotions took turns walking through my thoughts. One surprising realization soon became stunningly clear to me, though: Claire was *already* filling up the empty places inside me, places where anger and loneliness used to hide. Maybe if I held onto her more tightly, she'd push all that stuff right out of me forever.

Maybe she'd even replace it with love.

Chapter 30

Changing

LOVING YOU doesn't sound like such a chore to me....

I couldn't get Mitch's comment out of my head, because...well, because it didn't actually *want* to live in my head. Oh no, it kept trying to pack its bags, forward its mail, and move straight into my heart. As soon as the words left his mouth, my heart was clearing out space for them.

But no, of course I was trying to fight that move off like crazy. Believing that Mitch and I were going to end up in a loving relationship like the ones his brothers found would be a first-class ticket on the Heartbreak Express. That was especially true in the days following our talk on the futon the day his dad died, because grumpy loner Mitch was back. I have no idea precisely why—although, duh, grief—he'd gone from opening up to me and letting me offer him comfort to crawling right back inside of himself and treating me like a stranger. We were back at barnacle, basically. He stopped opening up to me and, as near as I could tell, stopped sleeping, too. He'd start in my bed each night, just like before. But then, instead of finding him wrapped around me in the morning, I was waking up alone. He moved to the futon at some point each night, then ran off to the gym as soon as he could shove his yummy body into workout clothes and get out the door.

I felt forgotten and disappointed, and I didn't really know what to do about it. At the very least, I had thought we were becoming friends, but my stupid heart began wanting more somewhere along the way. Here's the thing though: I don't think I was making it all up in my head. It sort of seemed—at times, anyway—like we were connecting beyond mere friendship. Like maybe we needed each other, and because of our connection, we were both somehow changing for the better.

And yeah, yeah—I know you're not supposed to start a relationship by trying to find all the ways you can change the other person. But that's not what I'm talking about here. It's more like that, in wanting to care for him and comfort him, I'd found myself also wanting more for myself. I suddenly realized I was working to consider my thoughts, censor my comments, and rethink my jokes, simply in an effort to wade out into his pool of grief and be the version of me he needed most. That's something I never thought I'd be able to do. Like ever. But Mitch made me want to be better than old Claire, I guess. And I thought maybe I was softening a few of his grumpy edges, too. Didn't he say being with me made things better? If that was the truth and not just, say, a flippant remark, then why was he working so hard to push me away and avoid me now? Because, therapist or not, I could tell he needed me now more than ever.

Unfortunately, I'd been working a lot of day shifts, which was messing with my ability to start researching master's programs. And more importantly, it was interfering with my desire to try to get my Mitch back. I had a feeling, though, that he was trying to avoid me anyway. He'd suddenly been taking a million walks, running out to the store to load up my fridge, and coming up with any other excuse he could find so that we were never in the apartment together for long. He even offered to take my car to get serviced. That one blew my mind.

"Mitch, c'mon," I said. "My car? Really? What's going on with you?"

"What do you mean?"

"I mean, what's *going on* with you?! You're clearly avoiding me and avoiding talking about why. Did I say something stupid to offend you? I mean, this is me we're talking about, so I realize the chances are good that I'm right here."

"No," he said, shaking his head and putting this stupid *I don't even know what language you're speaking* look of confusion on his face. Ugh. "I'm not avoiding you. We're friends, right? Friends don't let friends drive death mobiles that need, among other things, an oil change."

"Uh huh," I said. "Sure, fine, have it your way. Play dumb. Like I haven't noticed you've barely said two words to me since the day your father died. You opened up to me that night, but you've been shutting me out ever since. You just said we're friends, but you're sure not acting like we are. So I'll ask again— *what's...going...on?* Or are we gonna keep wasting time while stacking up dominoes of tension until they inevitably fall over and bury us? And of course there'll be no escaping them, what with that big stupid futon in the way."

Oops—I think that maybe my teensy tiny tact issue was back behind the wheel of my big mouth. Because as soon as I said those words and pushed him apparently a little too hard, I could tell the game was on.

Angry Mitch had never truly left the building.

Chapter 31

Truce

"YOU KNOW WHAT, Claire?" he said, ramping up in an instant. "News flash—nothing that's happening right now has anything to do with you. So stop pushing me and stop pretending it does."

"Right," I said. "So you lied just now, and we weren't actually becoming friends then? That doesn't really track, though, because I feel like I *was* part of what was happening during those morning cuddles and the hugs and the emotional dumpings. But hey, I'm just a simple waitress and don't understand complicated man stuff, right?"

"No, of course that's not what I mean. You've been great. I really appreciate that you let me crash here. But I'm going back to California, and you're staying here, and that's it. End of story."

"Why do you keep beating everyone, including yourself, over the head with that California crap?" Now I was getting fired up myself. "You keep waving that threat around. You're all, 'Ooh don't get attached because I'm leaving!' But anyone with eyes can see you don't actually want to go back. Stop being a big, closed-off baby and actually face your past for once! Reach out and grab the things you want from life!"

"Face my past?" he said. *'Face my past?!* Okay, stop right there because you don't know what you're talking about!"

"Sure I do, because you told me, back when you

were faking like we're friends. You still have a secret that you're holding onto, and it's eating you alive. Your brothers have begged and pleaded with you to tell them already so you can deal with whatever fallout it creates like a family. But no, not grumpy Mitch. You want to go hide in your apartment across the country, simmering in your anger and wondering why you can't find any happiness or human connections. But it's not that hard to figure out, and you're not as deep and mysterious as you think. I know why you're alone—*because you're choosing to be.* You act like absolutely everything that happened is your parents' fault, but when given a chance to fix things, you're choosing excuses and isolation and California. That's right, I'm saying it: You're choosing *you!*"

The phrase *The silence was deafening* is no joke, because Mitch didn't start yelling at me or stomping around and throwing things. He didn't walk out, either. He just…stared. I couldn't read the emotions on his face, either. His anger had melted away, I think. So had his broody avoidance. No…he just looked sort of taken aback. And thoughtful, I guess. I didn't figure I needed to say another word, because I'd let my anger and hurt launch way too many words already. Which meant that, clearly, the new and thoughtful Claire was a work in progress.

"We decided not to hold a funeral," he finally said. "I mean, why bother, right?"

"Yeah, I guess," I said, a little off balance at his sudden shift of topic. "Are you going to do anything at all?"

"Jake picked up the ashes today. We're going to meet at a restaurant tonight. Just, uh, come together one last time and call that the service, I guess."

"That'll be nice for you guys," I said, desperately wishing we were back at the "hugs as comfort" stage of our relationship. But of course I kept my arms at my side, right where they belonged. Y'know, since we weren't even friends, apparently. "Good idea."

"I, uh, I want you to be there."

"No you don't. You literally just got done saying I'm not a part of your life. And yeah, I used the word 'literally.' Because I'm annoying like that. Deal with it."

He shook his head. "I'm sorry for what I said, and I'm sorry for the way I've been treating you. You didn't deserve any of it, because yes, of course we're friends. You didn't read anything wrong. I just...I started panicking. Now that my dad's gone, there's nothing stopping me from telling my brothers exactly what happened. But I'm so scared it's going to devastate Max. I can't be the one to hurt him, I just can't. So I've been telling myself that maybe I don't *need* to tell him. Maybe I can just disappear, and you guys will return to your old lives, and everyone can forget I was ever here, you know?"

"Nope, I *don't* know," I replied immediately. "I don't know how I'd ever forget someone who sees me as clearly as you do and accepts me for exactly who I am. Your brothers are dying for you to stay, but—yeah, I might as well admit it out loud—I am, too. If you leave, you'll be missed, and that's the truth. And I'm sorry for what I said, too. I didn't mean to hurt you. See, I sort of have this issue where I lash out at people sometimes."

"Sounds familiar," he said, a few hints of the first smile I'd seen from him in days starting to rise at the corners of his mouth. "Come with me tonight? Please?"

"You sure? Last I heard this has nothing to do with me."

"Claire," he said, "I'm starting to realize it has

everything to do with you, and I don't know why I keep fighting it."

"Okay," I said with a nod. "I'll be there."

We didn't hug each other like we would have before, but we had taken a small step toward being friends again.

I guess it was going to have to be enough.

Chapter 32

Finally Ready

MY EMOTIONS had been bouncing and flipping like a kid on a trampoline for days. But something about Claire's heated words had reached out, taken me by the shoulders, and shaken me until clarity and sanity finally returned.

Maybe it was because she looked so beautiful, with her eyes flashing as brightly as her temper. Or maybe it was because this amazing, fiery woman had chosen to worry about *me*. And because of that, even as broken, lonely, and angry as she'd found me, I was very slowly and surely becoming someone new. Someone better. Someone who could share confidences and laughter and cuddles. Someone who maybe wasn't so angry or alone anymore.

I felt awful for taking out my panic and frustrations on her. I almost stopped communicating with her altogether, because I couldn't seem to find the right words to deal with my fears. Staying in New Jersey and making my life permanent there was terrifying, because it meant taking chances. Chances like telling Max and Jake the truth and telling Claire how much I was starting to care for her. And honestly, if I had any experience at all with the emotion, I might have even been able to call what I was feeling for her *love*. I wasn't completely sure, but what I did know was this: I was scared to reach out and grab it.

But I was equally scared not to.

Naturally, she had called me on it. After all, her bravery and honesty were a lot of what I lov…uh, liked so much about her. She called me on it, and it was the reality check I needed. Yes, we were friends. Yes, I needed her to come with me to the pseudo-funeral. And yes, it was time to tell my brothers everything I'd been holding back from them.

* * *

When Claire and I got to the restaurant, everyone else was already seated in the enormous booth; Max and Lily were on one side, and Jake and Melody on the other. That left Claire and me needing to split up. She sat next to Lily, and I scooted across from her, next to Jake. I was upset, at first, about not having her beside me, but being able to look into her face calmed me, too. That was good, because I was going to need her strength to get through that evening.

"I'm glad we were able to get together like this," I said after the server took our drink orders. "Especially since it might be the last time for a while."

"You're still heading back to California?" Jake asked, turning to shoot daggers of anger at me. "Are you serious? I thought you'd change your mind. But mostly I thought you'd finally try to lift some of your burdens by telling us everything before you leave. You trying to end up like me, stuck taking blood pressure medicine in your late twenties?"

"No, uh…no," I replied, nerves making my words rattle around in my head until they lost order and meaning. "I…I do think it's time. I'm…uh, I'm as ready as I'll ever be, I guess."

"F-finally!" Max said. "W-wait, you m-meant *now*, right? You'll tell us n-now?"

"Yeah, I think I have to," I said. "A wise person

told me today that I've been choosing this path. Choosing to be alone and in pain. But I can choose not to be, too."

"That was me, by the way," Claire said. "I'm the wise person. Just so we're all clear on that."

This made everyone chuckle, which helped to release some of the pressure. I gave her a smile, and she winked in return. Yeah, she knew exactly what she was doing with that joke. As always, she was right there, ready to support and help me.

The server came to deliver our drinks and take our food orders. I was grateful for the momentary distraction, but I could feel the panic start to bubble up again when she walked away. I scrubbed my palms on my jeans, furiously trying to wipe away the sweat and the nerves at the same time. It wasn't helping much, and I was starting to wonder if I was about to crawl straight out of my skin, when suddenly I could feel a hand gently touch my knee. I looked up to see Claire had subtly leaned forward so she could touch me. I covered her hand in my own and almost instantly felt my heart rate slow.

Everyone's eyes stayed locked on me. I closed my own and took a deep breath. When I opened them again, the first thing I noticed was the genuine concern on everyone's faces. Another thought struck me then— how had I ever felt alone when I had this much love and support in my life? All my old worries and feelings and fears suddenly felt foolish and small in the tidal wave of love currently washing over me.

"I didn't tell you everything when we were at Melody's," I began, "because I got scared."

"I'm glad you're admitting it," Jake said. "Apparently all we needed to do years ago was gather around a table with you. What's with you and table-side confessions?"

His joke had the same effect as Claire's, and again the tension in me—and around me—lowered.

"I don't know," I said. "All I know is that I love you guys, and I'm sorry I've been stuck in my head and tied up in fear. Max, I wanted to protect you from this truth so badly that it about killed me. Maybe not literally, like in Jake's case, but through isolation and anger. I'm sorry that it's going to take hurting you with this truth to set myself free. It...it feels selfish and wrong."

"J-just tell me, M-Mitch," Max said. "S-see this beautiful woman at m-my side? She'll h-help me through it. Wh-whatever it is, okay? P-please just set yourself f-free."

I nodded my head, squeezed Claire's hand, and finally started talking.

Chapter 33

The Secret

"I TOLD YOU GUYS the truth about that day," I began. "You took Max to the hospital, and I absolutely lost my mind on Dad. Kicks, punches, cursing…I didn't hold back."

Everyone's eyes were on me, but Claire's gave me the strength to keep going. Our gazes locked, and she nodded slightly, so I kept talking.

"And I already told you he shoved me against the wall and easily held me there. Pretty sure that moment has been my gym motivation every single day since. But anyway, then I started accusing him of any dumb thing I could think of and insulting him…honestly, I'm not sure why he didn't punch me, too. Well, no, that's not true, I guess. I think I *do* know why. Because in the middle of that verbal offensive I launched at him, I accidentally stumbled across the truth. When I did, I stunned him so badly that he let go, and I slid right to the floor. And he just stood there, hulking over me and shaking with anger. I honestly thought he was going to kill me."

"Wh-what did you say?!" Max asked. "What s-set him off?"

"I said that I couldn't believe how he was treating you," I replied, then stopped to steady my nerves. Claire squeezed my knee, and I took a deep breath again before continuing, although my words were slow and halting. I'm sure everyone at the table was ready to shake them out of me. But I'd spent a lot of energy and time avoiding this moment, and the words weren't suddenly going to slide out easily, not after so many years of being compressed inside me. "I said that I couldn't imagine how he could ever treat his flesh and blood that way. I said something like, 'What kind of monster punches his own kid in the head? You're a piece of garbage, and you know what, you're probably not even his real dad!' And then he got straight into my face so closely I could feel his breath on me, and he screamed, 'That's the thing, you brat, I'm not!'."

Max's eyes widened, and someone—Lily, I guess—gasped. The server showed up then with our meals, so my words had a chance to echo in the stunned silence while the plates were distributed.

"He's n-not my dad?" Max asked when she left. "Are you s-serious? But…w-wait, then wh-who is?"

"I don't know," I said, shaking my head. "I think that's a secret we've got to try to pull out of Mom, which probably won't be easy."

Max sat back, and all the shock I was afraid I'd inflict was right there in his eyes. But then, in a move that gave me a massive surprise of my own, he leaned forward and replaced the shock with a steely look of certainty.

"M-Mitch, I wish you h-hadn't suffered so long h-hiding this, because I think this news actually h-helps me," he said. "I'm k-kind of *glad* I'm n-not related to him, to b-be honest. It almost f-feels like a lottery p-prize. Although…I g-guess I'm not a C-Cruz, am I?"

"Yes you are," Jake said quickly, shooting an intense look across the table at him. "I've told you before I practically feel like a father to you. You've got the name Cruz not because you're his, but because you're *mine*."

A small, grateful smile crept onto Max's face,

where love and admiration for Jake were shining. I took a moment to appreciate what strong, amazing men my brothers were. Maybe if I'd been half as strong, I wouldn't have suffered, alone and angry, for so long. Maybe I would have called Dad out on all his stupid threats a long time ago. It made sense that they'd worked in intimidating a teenager. But how could I have let him win against the man I'd become? A wave of shame washed through me, and Claire must have been able to see its effects, because worry was pouring off her like an empathy waterfall.

"Yeah, Max, this changes nothing," I said finally, trying to turn my focus back on what actually mattered. Max's sense of self and security were what was important, and not my stupid regrets. "Half-brother, whole brother, who cares? We're brothers."

"Thanks," he said, nodding. "I l-love you, too, M-Mitch. And I'm s-so grateful that you s-stepped in to p-protect me. B-but keep going. Wh-what happened next?"

"Well, I said a bunch of dumb stuff about how I was going to find your real father so he could save you from Dad. And that's when the threats started. He said I wasn't going to embarrass him that way, and if I told a single soul, he'd make the punch that he gave you earlier look like a hug. I said there was no way I could hold in that secret forever, and that's when he said I would if I knew what was good for me. He said I'd better disappear and stay gone, taking what I knew with me. I agreed, but only if he agreed in exchange to leave you guys alone. If he didn't, I swore I'd tell the whole world his wife cheated on him, and then I'd call the cops and tell them about the punch. I might have even threatened to take out a billboard or two."

"Th-this still doesn't m-make sense, though," Max

said, his meal sitting untouched in front of him. "He only s-started abusing me wh-when I started s-stuttering. *That* was the t-trigger. It had everything to d-do with that, and n-nothing to do with this. I m-mean, come on—if it was about M-Mom having an affair, wh-why do I have m-memories of him p-playing with me and b-being nice to me b-before the stuttering started?"

"I don't know," I said, shaking my head again. "Maybe that's when she told him or something? I don't know. I'm sorry I don't have those answers."

"It can be genetic, though," Claire said. "I've got a few relatives who stuttered as kids, so that's how I know. Maybe it was simply a reminder to him that your genes and his genes weren't the same?"

"M-maybe," Max said, although he looked unconvinced.

"It seems like you three need to have a little talk with your mother," Melody said. "Based on what Jake's said about how out of touch she's getting, you should probably do it as soon as possible."

Jake nodded. "Yeah, Melody's right. I think we should do it in the morning, though, before she's had a chance to drink the day away, if that's even what she's been doing. We need her to be as lucid as possible."

"Then I guess we've got an interrogation to plan," I said.

So we agreed to descend upon our secretive mother the very next morning. Having even the simplest of plans and a way to move forward seemed to uncork the tension, and soon we were eating and chatting and laughing.

You know—the way a happy family would.

Chapter 34

Time and Silent Wishes

I WAS SO PROUD of Mitch for finally bursting free of the secrets that had shackled him for so long. The effort seemed to energize him at first, and he laughed and chatted and radiated a carefree energy that I don't think I'd ever seen from him before.

It wasn't until that evening, when we were lying quietly on our opposite sides of the bed, when these emotions crashed back down on him again.

"I messed up," he said, his voice wavering. "I spent all those years hiding information from Max, but it actually ended up helping him in the end. Only a total screw-up could have read the situation so wrong. I feel like I failed the most important test of my life. I failed *him.*"

"Sure, you could look at it that way if you wanted to dig deep for a reason to feel bad," I replied, hoping I was choosing the right words here, because I could almost tangibly feel the pain radiating from him. I desperately wished we were back at the hugging stage of our odd friendship, but things still felt tentative between us. "But you're digging really deep, and you're conveniently forgetting a whole lot of truth. *This* Max isn't the boy you were trying to protect all those years ago. I wasn't around to see it, but from what I understand, he fell straight down into a trauma-filled pit after the day you described, right?"

I waited for him to acknowledge what I'd said, but

his silence told me more than his words could have. He was lost and sinking quickly himself, and I was desperate to reach out my hand to save him.

I decided to continue with, "He did. That young boy who was so traumatized that he couldn't speak for years is who you wanted to save. That boy couldn't have handled one more hint of shocking news. So your sacrifice gave him and Jake the gift of *time,* which was what they desperately needed. Max would one day be able to work through his issues and emerge strong and resilient. The stronger Max was only possible because of the sacrifices and choices *you* made for him. You did what you had to do. That's it, Mitch. That's the simple truth of it. You took on the burden of this secret, and you gave up time with your family so it could happen. *Of course* you've been angry and lonely. But that's because it wasn't fair to you. None of it was fair to any of you. But stop right there with whatever accusations you're flinging at yourself. You made Max's recovery possible. He was only able to accept hearing this news so easily today because of you."

"You're twisting it to make me sound good," he said. "I'm no one's hero. Jake's the one who helped Max, not me."

"I said it before, but I guess you didn't hear me," I said. "You gave them the time they needed. Max took *years* to recover, years that were a present from you. So it wasn't only a Jake thing. Yeah, of course he played a huge role. But it took all three of you working together and playing your individual parts to help Max survive his childhood. Then Lily came along and wrapped him up in all her awesomeness, too. But it took time for her entrance into his life. So that's what you gave him; it's what you gave *both* of them. Can't you see how true that is? I'm not just sugar-coating everything to be nice. And since when am I known for all the syrupy sweet things I say, anyway? Don't forget who you're dealing with here. It's me. Claire of the truth bombs, remember? I don't lie to be nice. Claire's gonna Claire."

This bit of silliness achieved what I'd hoped, and I heard him chuckle.

"I don't think I could have gotten through this without you. I'm so sorry I tried to push you away. You've somehow gone from enemy to best friend inside of a month. It's kind of impressive, really."

"I get that a lot," I said, hoping to hear his laugh again. He didn't let me down, the deep rumble filling up lots of places inside me that used to be clogged with junk like worries about my inability to connect with people. I may drive everyone else crazy, but Mitch seemed to like me just the way I was.

I sent a few silent wishes into the air then. Wishes that Mitch and his brothers would finally find peace. And wishes that he and I could move past mere friendship one day. I know that the second one was a bit of a tall order, but I desperately wanted it, nevertheless. Somewhere along the way, when I'd been busy making the journey from being his enemy to his best friend, he'd been hard at work stealing my heart.

"I meant what I said: I'm sorry for shutting you out," he said, turning his head toward me now. "So can we pretend it's morning?"

I thought about making a dumb joke about panini presses or human burritos or whatever. But New Claire seemed to be in charge, and she wasn't interested in being funny. Nope, not when an amazing guy like Mitch was looking for comfort in her arms.

"Get over here," I told him, rolling right into his embrace.

Chapter 35

Confronting Mom

"HAS MOM been any better lately?" I asked. I felt guilty that I'd avoided seeing her when Jake still was checking on her daily.

After I moved back, I decided I couldn't let him shoulder everything anymore. And I chose not to dwell on why I used the phrase *"after* I moved back" rather than *"if* I moved back." Part of the issue was that I needed to get back to work, something I hadn't been able to focus on since I arrived. If I kept turning down jobs, I'd be looking for a new way to pay my bills soon. I needed to go back, whether my subconscious liked it or not.

"Nah, she's the same," he replied from his spot behind the wheel. Once again, we were crammed into his pickup. "Not sure this is going to get us the answers we want."

"I g-guess, in a way, it d-doesn't matter," Max said. "She either t-told the guy and he d-didn't care about me, or he n-never knew I existed. And if he n-never knew, is there any p-point in searching for him n-now, after all th-these years?"

I shrugged. "Maybe, maybe not. Maybe he was as big of a jerk as Dad, or he could be this great guy out there somewhere who would love to learn he has an awesome son like you. But we're getting ahead of ourselves here. There's no guarantee she'll even own up to it. If she denies everything, I'm not sure what else we could do."

"Yeah," Jake said, pulling into the driveway, throwing the truck into park, and exhaling a weary sigh. "That's where I'm at with this. I think there's a huge chance she either pretends not to remember or legitimately doesn't. And there's also a chance this was all in his head. Maybe he only accused her of cheating because he was so very offended that any son of his might have a speech problem. We all believed it when you finally told us, and clearly you bought what he was selling during that confrontation, Mitch. But he might have made himself believe it, just because he was a piece of garbage. We have to consider that possibility, too."

"Very true," I replied, "and of course I never thought of that back then. I don't remember him being a great actor, though. And I think he fully believed it, for what that's worth. I guess this comes down to Mom. But before we head down this road, Maxwell, you're *sure* you want to know? We could always leave it alone and keep the truth buried in the past."

His hands were twisting and fidgeting in his lap. "I know I j-just said it d-doesn't matter, but that's not t-true. I n-need to know."

Jake and I looked at each other and nodded. That's all that mattered, I thought, as we climbed out. This was all about what he wanted and needed, and I honestly couldn't blame him. I'd probably want to know, too.

*　　*　　*

Mom was every bit as flustered as we guessed she'd be when the three of us showed up. It took quite a while for us to convince her that no, we didn't need anything to drink, and no, she didn't need to make us any breakfast, and no, she looked fine and didn't need to go change.

When we got her settled, an awkward silence fell over us, and I regretted that we hadn't talked about how to approach this conversation. We'd dissected whether or not to do it, but not *how* to do it. When the moment arrived, it was clear we'd made a misstep.

But this was my secret, and I was the one who got this ball rolling by guessing the truth—or at least Dad's version of it, as Jake had pointed out. I decided that getting us started was on my shoulders.

"Mom," I said, aiming to be both direct and gentle, "a long time ago, Dad told me something about you and Max. Can I ask whether what he said was true?"

"Oh, I don't know," she said. "Why are we talking about the past?"

"Mom, I've kind of been stuck in the past ever since he told me this. It's been haunting me, I guess you could say. I need you to help set me free."

"Oh, Mitchell, you were always so dramatic," she said, as though that were the truth. I'd hardly been a dramatic child, but maybe she was referring to the dramatic way I left.

"Mom, please. I need you to tell us if Dad was lying when he said that Max isn't his son."

"Mitchell!" she said, her voice sharp and reprimanding, in a tone that only mothers can pull off successfully. "Why would you say such a thing?"

"I didn't say it," I reminded her. "Dad did. So please tell me: *Why* would he say such a thing?"

"I don't know," she said, shaking her head and starting to fuss with a throw pillow wedged next to her in the old recliner. "I can't begin to imagine."

"Mom," Jake said, "no one is going to think you're a bad person if this is true. You can be honest with us. Don't you think Max deserves to know?"

"Max?" she said. "He was such a sweet boy."

"M-Mom?" Max said, shooting us a puzzled look, "I'm right here."

"Max?" she said, "Oh yes, of course you are, dear."

Jake blew out an exasperated breath, and Max looked upset, so I decided to try again.

"Mom, when we were little, you worked at a big office building, right? I don't remember what kind of business it was, or even what you did there. But I think you took Jake and me to meet your boss once or something."

"Insurance," she replied, nodding. "Yes, that's right. I was at the receptionist's desk. Such a lovely company. Mr. Collins was always wonderful to me."

"You were there quite a while," I said, glancing over at Jake now. *Mr. Collins?* Maybe it was a classic "affair with the boss" thing? "Were you and Mr. Collins close?"

"Close?" she said, sounding dumbfounded now. "How close do you think a man in his sixties would be with a young receptionist?"

"Okay, so did you make any other friends there?" I asked, letting her comment and any possible snarky replies float away.

I don't know where I was going with this line of questioning, exactly. But our parents had never been social; I don't remember either of them having any friends at all. If she had an affair, it wasn't with someone she met when she was out with a bunch of girlfriends or at neighborhood parties or couples' outings or anything else along those lines. We'd been fairly insulated, and honestly that probably fed into Dad's ability to terrorize Max for so long.

"Friends?" she said. "Don't be silly. We couldn't all

have lunch together. Someone had to answer the phones, after all. The whole group of them would go out and have these long lunches, and I always said I just didn't know where they got the money or the time for it. I mean, really, can you imagine?"

I shook my head, and Jake's face mirrored my frustration. That hadn't gotten us very far, and I was out of ideas about where she could possibly have met someone.

"S-so you ate l-lunch at your desk?" Max asked, not as ready to bang his head against a wall as I already was, apparently. "Alone?"

"Sure, of course," she said. "If too many calls came in at once, or if I was in the middle of a bite, sometimes he'd help me out, though."

"Who helped?" Jake said, shooting a meaningful look at Max and me. "Who helped you?"

"Why, Colin did, of course," she said, looking up at us then with an amused look on her face before she swung her gaze directly at Max. "*You* helped me, didn't you?"

Chapter 36

Surprises and Reactions

I HAD THE DAY OFF for the first time in quite a while, and I really should have used the time to do laundry. Or clean my apartment. Or get a haircut. Honestly, there were a billion things I should have done that day, but somehow *Worry about Mitch* floated right to the top of my to-do list and refused to let me cross it off or even multitask. So yeah, I really dug into that job and gave it all my energy. Lily was at work, or I would have been next door trying to see if she'd heard anything yet. Part of me was dying to at least text Mitch and check in, especially once the morning turned to afternoon. But I held back. If he wanted me all up in the middle of it, he would have invited me to go, right?

I was elbow-deep in a bag of cheese curls that was functioning as both my lunch and dinner when Mitch finally walked through the door. He looked golden with a deep tan and glow of sweaty-yet-sexy exertion, like he'd spent the afternoon frolicking on the beach or something.

"Uh, why do you look like you just wrapped up your shift on the lifeguard stand?" I asked, a cheese curl in my fingers and frozen in the air in front of my mouth as I assessed him.

"Moving on from Doritos, I see," he said, kicking off his shoes and sitting on the edge of the futon where I was currently sprawled.

"Corn, potato, cheese…I need to eat from all the

food groups to maintain a healthy and balanced diet," I said. "Geez, Mitch, didn't you learn anything in health class?"

"Missed that day, I guess," he said, not revealing a hint of a smile or amusement at my dumb joke, something he typically had time for no matter what. I took it for the clue it was—their day hadn't been easy. "Listen, we're heading over to Melody's. Want to come?"

"Ooh, like a date?" I said, resorting to my old standby of dropping jokes in the middle of any kind of mood or situation. Guess I wasn't evolving as much as I thought, and I regretted the words the minute they left my mouth. I regretted them even harder when I saw his reaction, which was this look that somehow was equal parts surprise and horror.

"Uh...a date?" Mitch said, looking downright trapped now. "No...I...it's not...I mean, we're not—"

"Dude, breathe," I said, mortification crawling up my neck now. I was suddenly especially embarrassed, for some reason, about the thick crust of cheese dust on my fingers and the sloppy sweats I was wearing. I felt childish and kind of gross, and I would've crawled inside the bag of cheese curls if that had been an option. "You know me, I was just joking. I know I'm not your ditzy model type, so move on. What's happening at Melody's?"

"Not my type?" he asked, but now my embarrassment was morphing into irritation, and I kind of wanted to punch his beautifully perfect face.

"Focus, Mitch. I've been dying to know what happened today. Is that what this gathering is about?"

"Okay, yeah. We just wanted to talk about our trip to Mom's, and we figured it'd be easiest to get together and only go over it once. So come on, you in?"

"Yeah, just give me a minute to change," I replied, fleeing the futon. I flipped the bag onto the kitchen counter, then headed to the bathroom to clean up a little. Well, okay—and to try to choke back the hurt that his reaction caused. If I'd ever had any dreams or wishes about us being a couple one day, he'd very effectively ground them into a fine powder in that moment. My heart was splintering in two, and the pain surprised me. I knew I was allowing myself to get too attached to him, I guess. But I didn't comprehend until that moment just how much pain I was going to be in when he left.

I tried to fake like everything was cool on the drive to Melody's, but he kept shooting questioning looks at me that I was working overtime to ignore. Like he didn't know, at the bare minimum, that he embarrassed me.

The big jerk.

*   *   *

When we got there, I made a beeline for Lily, who was sitting next to Max. Melody pulled some chairs out of the kitchen to accommodate anyone who couldn't find a seat, and I ignored the questioning looks Mitch was sending my way. He probably thought I should be at his side, holding his hand and helping him through this. And I guess, as the friends we'd become, I should have been open to that. But I was feeling raw and embarrassed; I was in no mood to play along, whether he needed me or not. He was leaving soon anyway, right? So I was doing him a favor. He needed to practice dealing with everything alone like I always did.

"So, you're killing us," Melody said. "What happened? And why'd it take so long?"

"The conversation wasn't all that long," Mitch said.

"But we spent the rest of the day fixing some things around her house. The windows needed caulking, and the yard was wildly out of control despite Jake's attempts to stay on top of it. We basically turned into a handyman work crew."

"That was nice of you," Lily said, squeezing Max's hand furiously. "But, seriously, tell us about the talk."

"She's gone downhill fast," Jake began. "So we didn't get as much out of her as we would've liked. I called her doctor when those two were working on the windows. I made an appointment that we're going to have to force her to go to, based on how she's been acting, basically since Dad died."

"Maybe it's her way of dealing with the grief," I suggested, immediately regretting calling attention to myself. Mitch's gaze locked with mine, and I could see his mind was whirring away, probably trying to figure out how to get me to stop acting weird. I wanted the same thing, too, though, so I just shrugged at him.

"Maybe," Jake replied. "But it was alarming enough to at least make the appointment. She's confused and still doesn't seem to understand who Max is."

"So that's it?" Melody asked. "It was a dead end?"

"N-not exactly," Max said. "She keeps c-calling me C-Colin. Turns out she used to w-work with a man named C-Colin who was n-nice to her. We're g-guessing here, and only because she k-keeps confusing me with him, th-that he m-might be my father."

"Worked where?" Lily asked.

"Honor Insurance," Jake said. "That big building downtown with the blue mountains on the sign? Her boss was Mr. Collins. That little nugget is basically the only other clue we got out of her, unless you want to hear about her coworkers' long lunches."

"Colin?" I asked, my heart suddenly Irish step dancing in my chest. "Colin...Chambers?"

"We didn't get a last name," Mitch said. "Oh, wait, are you related to a Colin who worked there?"

"My dad?" I said, feeling like the words were choking me. "Yeah, we're related."

As those words left my mouth, Max turned to me, his eyes wide and his mouth dropping open.

Chapter 37

Reeling

NO ONE KNEW what to say. The tension was so thick in the room that I felt like it was choking me. Or maybe it was the tears I was battling back, something I almost never have to worry about, even when I'm truly upset. Tears simply have never been my go-to emotional release—that's what inappropriate comments and snark are for, after all—but I felt throttled by them as I watched Max slowly close his mouth, his eyes still riveted on my face.

"I g-guess I d-don't even kn-know this k-kind of s-stuff about you, but wh-where is your d-dad?" he asked, his emotional response clearly as debilitating as mine, since his stuttering suddenly became more pronounced than I'd ever heard it. We were getting a glimpse of the old, pre-Lily Max.

"He died years ago," I said. "Heart attack. He was sitting right at his desk at good-old Honor Insurance."

Again, my comment was met with silence, and the tears I was fighting were launching a similar assault on Max now. I could see them glistening at the edges of his brown eyes.

"I'm sorry," I said, furious with myself. That was how I chose to tell this kindhearted soul that a man who might have been his father was dead, and that he'd therefore never have the chance to know him? "Max, seriously, please forgive me. I should have said that more gently."

"Everybody chill out," Jake said. "We don't know anything for sure. It could be a total coincidence. I mean, come on, there had to have been more than one guy named Colin working there. That building is huge."

"His boss was Mr. Collins," I said, my voice sounding wooden. "He mostly grew out of it, but when he got very emotional or upset, my dad's old childhood stutter would make an appearance. His brother and father had both mostly grown out of theirs, too, so that's why I knew it was genetic, although Chad and I never had one."

"Right, okay, so the coincidences are stacking up," Jake said, glancing over at Melody now. No one else seemed to know what to do or say, and I think that maybe they were giving me a minute to process everything. As though having one or two long seconds of silence would be enough to soak in the knowledge that your dead father wasn't the man you thought he was. So yeah, I didn't know how to react, either. And I definitely didn't know how to release everyone from the claws of awkwardness that clutched us. For once, I didn't have an easy joke or quip ready to go.

"Claire-bear," Lily said, her voice very gentle and calming as she took my hand with the one not clutching Max's, "I don't really remember much about your dad. It's been too long, and he avoided us during sleepovers and stuff. I don't even remember much of what he looked like, to be honest. So I guess that means you're the only one here who knows the answers to any part of this. Do *you* think it's possible? I mean, you and Chad don't exactly look like Max."

Her comments helped lift some of my fog, and for the first time I realized what this all meant: Max could be my *brother.* At that thought, I looked into his face and worked to find my father's features. I guess the nose and jawline were similar, as were the brown eyes, but he definitely wasn't an exact copy of my dad.

"I mean, I can see some similarities," I said. "The nose. The jaw. But otherwise...."

"I don't know, because you two don't exactly look alike," Mitch said, a worried tone to his voice that made me turn to him. He was clearly upset and frustrated. My earlier pain from his rejection was still there after all, even though it was now buried under this new layer of pain. In the end, however, I simply turned my gaze back to Max.

"Chad and I look like my mom," I said. "Dad used to joke about it. Ha ha, that's so funny in retrospect. Good one, Dad. So glad you could make jokes about us looking like the mailman while you were off making babies at work."

"I'm s-sorry," Max said, looking stricken, which made me feel like a jerk for hurting him again. After all, he was the only other person in that room who could even guess how much I was suffering then. His world was on fire too, after all.

"No, *I'm* sorry," I replied. "I didn't mean anything by it. You know how I get with the sarcasm. You wouldn't know it from how I'm acting right now, but it's something I've been trying to work on. Anyway, if it's true, Max, having you for a brother would be one of the best things that could ever happen to me."

He offered me a little smile, and that's when I saw it—*the smile*. Max suddenly *did* look like my dad, so much so that I honestly kind of wondered why I'd never seen it before.

"I...I need to go," I announced, jumping up and walking straight to the front door before anyone could even react.

"Claire, wait," I heard Mitch say as he chased after me.

Moments later, as I opened the door to my car—and purposely left the passenger side locked—Mitch jogged up to the car. He came in hot with "tame the wild animal" energy, his hands up in what was probably supposed to be a soothing gesture. "We came together, remember? We'll go home and talk and hug and all the other roomie stuff we do."

Part of me wanted every single bit of the comfort he was offering. But the truth of the matter was that my heart wanted *more* than what he was offering, too. And I no longer wanted to walk that fine line with him. Friends don't cuddle in bed. Screw that. Screw him.

"Get a ride from someone else," I told him, climbing in and driving away without looking at his gorgeous face again. I couldn't take him and his family and all their secrets anymore. It was too much. Just way, way too much.

*   *   *

I drove to my mom's house, relieved that Chad's Jeep wasn't in the driveway. I went inside and immediately startled about five years off my mom's life because I forgot to text first or to make a bunch of noise like I normally do.

"Oh, Claire, you scared me!" she said. "Hey, baby, what's wrong?"

I sat on the couch next to her, leaned into her offered hug, and finally released those tears.

Chapter 38

Space and Status Quo

I WAS IN UTTER SHOCK as I walked back into Melody's house, my thoughts like a marching band inside my skull. *Claire?* Was it possible that this incredibly strong, independent, and insanely funny woman was Max's sister? My *brother's* sister?! That thought gave me a small panic attack. Did that also mean Claire and *I* were related?!

Did it...?

I paused as I stepped inside the door, closing it behind me and then leaning there a moment, taking the time to diagram a family tree in my head. That alone told me two things: One, I was an idiot, and two, no, of course we weren't related. We shared a sibling—maybe—but not a parent.

Actually, I guess it taught me *three* things, because what would it matter if Claire and I were related anyway? That is, unless I had real feelings for her and planned to pursue more than mere friendship with her? I'd been telling myself all along that we were nothing but friends and that's how it'd stay, especially since my future plans were so murky. But…well, I was starting to wonder if staying merely friends was even possible. Somewhere along the way, I think things had changed.

Maybe it happened when I realized that being with her was such a calm in the storm. Take, for example, the fact that I could actually sleep in her arms. Or maybe it was because she could always, *always* make me laugh. Or maybe it was in the way she helped me—by merely putting her hand on my knee—when releasing my secrets unleashed a hurricane inside me.

Still…I was confused. I didn't want a long-distance relationship, and I didn't want to lead her on or make her believe I was something more than I actually was. Or, for that matter, that I had enough inside me to offer her. I'd been broken a very, very long time. Dumping a secret or two sure wasn't going to fix what was damaged, and now I'd managed to mess up her life too in the aftershocks of my own messy truths.

She asked me earlier if we were going on a date. What I should have done was be courageous—like *she* always is—and own up to the fact that, yes, I had feelings for her that seemed to be bursting out of me. But I didn't feel like I should do anything about them until I figured myself out first.

Instead of raw honesty, however, I'd bellyflopped into a pool of awkward babble, and in doing so I'd definitely hurt her. Now she was out there alone, raw, and vulnerable. That meant she didn't feel she could turn to me when she needed me the most. My stupid panic and indecision and self-doubt had cost us both, and now here we were, back to strangers.

Hopefully not back to enemies, though.

"Mitch, is she okay?" Jake asked, catching sight of me still leaning against the front door.

"No," I replied, his comment jerking me out of my inner turmoil and leaving me feeling unbalanced. "She sped off. Wouldn't talk."

Melody was nodding. "I'm sure she just needs time to process all of this. I think *all* of you need time to process this. It's been one revelation after another lately, so of course it's going to take an emotional toll."

"I c-can't believe any of it," Max said, shaking his head. "It's c-crazy."

"It makes a *little* sense," I said, walking into the living room to join them. "You and Claire both have wicked senses of humor. You're both strong and brave and incredible. I don't know Chad, though, so who knows about him."

"I *told* Claire I'd end up with her brother!" Lily suddenly said, looking excited when the realization struck. "I was just confused about which one for a while!"

"Lily used to draw little hearts around Chad's name in all her notebooks," I said when I noticed the confusion on Melody and Jake's faces.

"T-too soon," Max said. "I've always k-kinda hated that g-guy, first because L-Lily liked him, and s-second because he b-broke her heart. And now that j-jackwagon is my b-brother."

"Maybe," Lily said. *"Maybe* he's your brother. But he didn't break my heart, because it was never his in the first place. He embarrassed me, that's it. Big difference. My heart has always been, and will only ever be, yours."

Melody sighed and Jake wore a satisfied, fatherly look of contentment as Max and Lily followed up her sweet speech with a kiss. But for me, watching all this made pain twist in my chest. I thought again about how I'd messed things up with Claire.

Lily said that Max always held her heart. Was that how I felt about Claire? My mind again scrolled through memories of her and the time we'd spent together. She always challenged and surprised me. She always made me laugh. She supported and comforted me, yet she was no pushover. She was smart enough to know her own faults, and brave enough to work on improving herself. She was beautiful and…well, yeah okay, who was I kidding here? She held my heart.

Pain and remorse wrestled for dominance inside me, right along with a fair share of doubt. What was holding me back from embracing her *and* a future together right there in New Jersey, where I should have been all along? I mean, yeah, there were the simple logistics of dealing with the apartment, but it wasn't a big deal. No, something else had me frozen and unable to shed my indecision and isolation. Until I could figure that out, I guess nothing would change. Nothing *could* change.

And it was clear she needed time to deal with the possible revelations about her father, anyway. Maybe I simply needed to back off and give her space. I decided then and there that I would stay on the futon that night.

Once I landed on the plan to maintain the status quo—and to try to give Claire some space before attempting to mend the broken threads of our friendship—I felt better. After all, Claire and Max both needed me. This wasn't the time to be making any big changes or declarations. We all just needed to chill out and breathe.

Because if I didn't know anything else, I knew this: In just a few short days, we'd all weathered enough secrets and revelations to last a lifetime.

Chapter 39

Stepping Back

I DIDN'T TELL MY MOM about my father's affair that night. I mean, come on, I didn't even know it was the truth anyway. But my mom still loved and missed him, and I couldn't imagine ever twisting and tainting those memories for her. What purpose would it serve? It certainly wouldn't bring him back or help him explain the choices he'd made. So even if Max and I matched up in a DNA test one day, I was certain I should keep that secret from her permanently.

Chad was another story. Mostly I thought he should know, if we were able to one day *prove* it was true. But he had a big, stupid, flappy mouth. I wouldn't want him to tell Mom, either accidentally or purposely. So maybe he wouldn't need to know, either. I just wasn't sure at that point, which meant I needed to think about it more.

I needed to think about a lot of things, really. Like the fact that I'd gone and fallen in love with a man I had no chance to be with. For one thing, he clearly didn't return the feelings. And he obviously had zero idea what he wanted out of life, feelings for me or not, now that his main identity wasn't wrapped up in being everyone's official Vault of Secrets.

The pain about Mitch was almost more than I could deal with in light of the revelations about my dad. If those revelations were true, then I was angry and disappointed in the father I'd always admired and revered. I *hated* that he might have cheated on my mom, but I think even more than that, I hated that he hadn't saved Max from Mitch and Jake's creepy dad. Maybe if he'd stepped in and yanked Max out of that situation, we could have grown up together. Max and Lily would probably have been childhood sweethearts, and Max never would have suffered the way he did. Although, I guess I was also forgetting my mom's potential suffering in that otherwise pretty picture.

Speaking of my mom, she wanted to know why I was sobbing all over her, of course. I couldn't tell her everything, but I knew she'd understand about the man trouble. So I explained the tears away by spilling my broken heart, then I gladly accepted when she offered to let me stay with her as long as I needed.

After we finally said good night, I went upstairs to get ready for bed. I knew the minute Mitch returned to the apartment, because worried texts started lighting up my phone when I was hunting for Mom's stash of new toothbrushes.

Mitch: Where are you?

I thought about replying, but I was busy with the whole toothbrush thing, plus I had solid plans to crawl into my childhood bed and watch funny videos online. Clearly, I had no time to engage. He was probably mad because his human pillow wasn't there, ready to serve his every sleeping need.

Several minutes later, he tried again.

Mitch: Claire, please, I'm worried about you. I know you're upset, but please at least let me know you're alive. I'm about two seconds away from calling local hospitals, filing a missing-persons report, and hiring search-and-rescue dogs.

I rolled my eyes and typed out a reply.

Me: I'm at my mom's house. I'm fine. Celebrate, you've got the place to yourself.

Mitch: Did you tell her? She okay?

Me: Of course I didn't tell her. Even if we prove it's true, I'll probably never tell her. Her love for him is too big, even after all this time. She never needs to know.

Mitch: I'm sorry you're in pain, and I'm sorry I had a part in it. You have to know I never wanted to hurt you.

My eyes flew open in shock as I read and re-read his last comment. Was he talking about hurting me because his secrets led to this revelation about my dad cheating on my mom? Or was he talking about the whole dating fiasco earlier, and his stupid, rambling response to it? I read his words again: *You have to know I never wanted to hurt you.*

His meaning was suddenly extremely clear. This new realization blasted pain in my heart, which then radiated wildly throughout my body. No, that comment wasn't about my dad; although, sure he probably never meant to take me out with the shrapnel from his secret. But yes, the words were otherwise very stark and clear. He was telling me he never meant for me to get attached to him. He hadn't put any effort into being so sizzling hot and irresistible. He hadn't intended for any jokes to be innuendoes or for hugs to one day turn into passionate embraces. And he definitely never meant for me to get all silly and sloppy and fall in love with him.

Mitch: Claire, you still there? What can I do to help? You've been right by my side through all of this, and now it's my turn. What do you need?

What did I need? *What did I need?!* That was a joke. I needed to still believe my dad was an honorable man who loved his family, but who also wouldn't abandon a son who was being abused. I needed to stop hurting. And I needed Mitch to love me back.

What I *didn't* need was more pain, and talking to him or seeing him was a direct route toward a lot more suffering. What I needed most, I guess, was to cut him right out of my life.

For a juvenile moment, I considered blocking his number on my phone. But I dismissed that urge as soon as it appeared. I just couldn't do it, especially since it was looking like our families were intertwined. I wouldn't be able to avoid him forever, but I could sure do it for a while.

Me: Nah, I'm fine. You know me. Nothing knocks me down for long. The best thing you can do for me is to give me space. I'm going to stay with my mom. The apartment is yours until you go back to California. Good luck with everything.

After I hit SEND, I turned off the phone and clicked off the light.

Then, for the second time that day, I let the tears and misery overtake me.

Chapter 40

Anger and Brotherly Advice

IT TURNS OUT there's something way worse than being enemies who launch bombs at each other in the form of cutting comments and snippy replies. Worse than that by far, I found out the hard way, is silence and indifference. Unfortunately, it took landing in the middle of Claire's dismissive avoidance for me to figure that out. It was only then that I realized all those snappy comments and angry retorts had been a whole lot of chemistry; she'd single-handedly electrified me with it and, in doing so, had brought me back to life. As a result, I was lost without her, and I had no idea what to do about it.

Looking back, it was very easy to see that I hadn't been truly alive before she crashed into the middle of my lonely existence. Look at the way I'd been sleepwalking for months through that pathetic non-relationship with Tifanee. Cutting her out of my life had felt, at most, like a relief. But having Claire do the same thing to me? I couldn't believe how much it hurt or how desperately I missed her. I found myself wanting to sleep on her side of the bed, clutching a bag of chips and listening to sad songs.

Yeah, I was a hot mess without her.

* * *

After I spent a few days moping and sending texts that went unanswered, my brothers must have had enough of my depression, because they called me on it while we were in Jake's truck, on our way to Mom's house again.

"What's going on with you?" Jake asked. "And don't say it's nothing, because anyone could see that something's bugging you. But please tell me you don't have more secrets."

"No," I said, with a rueful chuckle. "Well, I mean, maybe one."

Both my brothers' heads swiveled, and their twin looks of horror made me laugh again.

"Chill out," I said. "It has nothing to do with either of you."

"So wh-what does it have to d-do with, then?" Max asked.

I pretty much had to answer since I was trapped in the truck with them. Jake had tried a few times to get Mom to tell him more about the mysterious Colin, but he'd gotten nowhere. We were planning to do some more work around her house that day, but we also wanted to see if Max could get her to talk. Seeing him made her think about Colin, after all. It was clear that Max's presence likely held the key to unlocking the mystery. Lily said Claire was open to doing a DNA test, but we wanted to try the cheaper, and hopefully simpler and faster, route first.

"Uh, I messed up, I guess," I finally said. "I hurt Claire, and I don't know how to fix it."

Max turned a deadly glare at me. "H-hurt her *how?*"

"Whoa, relax," I said, remembering this was possibly his sister we were talking about. I needed to keep that in mind, especially in the face of the fiery reaction he just gave me. "I just…I might have gone and fallen for her or something. But I'm such a hot mess that I don't know *what* I want. I don't really have anything to offer her, anyway. She made an off-hand comment several days ago about going on a date, and I tripped all over myself denying it. Now she's avoiding me, and I just…I just miss her, you know? But what am I supposed to do about it? It's not like I can take a magic wand and make all my problems go away."

I thought I'd get some sympathy—and I was counting on some good advice to come right along with it—but what I got instead were some very angry reactions.

"You're an idiot," Jake said, throwing the truck into park in the driveway and turning an irritated look toward me.

"H-how are you w-worse at c-communicating than I am?" Max asked, shaking his head, disgust rolling off him. "Dude, it's t-time for some s-serious self-reflection."

"What?!" I said, instantly defensive. "Look, I wasn't *trying* to hurt her. Of course I wasn't. But I can't lead her on, either. I don't think there's anything inside me worth loving at this point. I've been alone for too long. I've been angry too long. I'm protecting her here, so don't get all judgey about it. I need advice, not more problems."

"M-my advice is to at l-least tell her th-that stupid stuff about b-being unlovable," Max said after a pause to reflect and consider. "T-trust me, I've b-been there with those f-feelings. But g-guess what? L-Lily loves me anyway. If you have even a s-slight chance of f-finding what I have with L-Lily, then you better g-grab it."

"Max is right," Jake said. "Melody and I had a tough road to travel, too, with all the fallout from her abusive marriage. But we talked it out, and loving her— and being loved by her—is the best thing that ever happened to me."

"I guess," I said, knowing the words were weak even as I let them limply roll out of my mouth. But my brothers couldn't possibly understand. They hadn't been alone as long as I had. They'd always had each other, and that support had made a difference in their lives and in the ways they'd been able to recognize love when they saw it, then reach out and embrace it. Everything for me was…different.

"I don't know her that well," Jake said, opening the door to get out, "but from what I do know, she's one tough lady. I think you're underestimating her. If she got in a fight with a grizzly, my money would be on her. So stop acting like you're protecting a delicate flower who can't make up her own mind."

Jake stopped to take a breath as Max and I chuckled about the bear line. I mean…he wasn't wrong. Claire's tough.

"And you're wrong about something else, too," he went on. "You think of yourself as this super angry person, but I haven't seen that guy in a really long time. Think back and be honest with yourself: When's the last time rage filled you up so full that you couldn't breathe? Ever since you got here, and you and Claire collided into each other's lives, just how angry have you honestly been? Don't answer me right now, but think about it. My guess is that you're going to have a hard time coming up with more than one or two examples of this constant anger you claim to carry around like a security blanket."

When he'd finished delivering his thoughtful and impassioned speech, he climbed out of the cab. Stunned, I did the same, with my thoughts stirring in my head and keeping me off balance. Was there truth to what he said? Was all that anger really gone?

Reeling, I followed my brothers up the front stairs and into our childhood home. We found our mother out back fussing with a bird feeder. It was the first normal thing I'd seen her do since my return. She'd always loved her backyard birds.

"Hey Mom," Jake said, and I waved when she glanced up at us. "Look who Mitch and I brought with us. It's Colin…wait, what's your last name, Colin?"

"F-Fitzgibbon," Max said, pulling a name out of the air. "C-Colin Fitzgibbon."

"Don't be silly!" Mom said, turning a smile toward him now. "Colin, you're always so funny."

"Okay, th-then what's m-my real n-name?" he asked, and a tense sizzle of expectation passed through the three of us. Could it really be this easy to pull the truth from her?

"I always just call you Colin or Col, naturally," she said, fluttering her hand at him in what had to be a flirty gesture she used to use. Meanwhile, the three of us exchanged tense looks. "But of course, Mr. Collins demands formality," she continued. "It's always 'Mrs. Cruz,' and never just 'Hazel'."

"What does he c-call me?"

"Oh Colin," she said, looking at him like he was being dense. "You know the answer to that question. He calls you 'Mr. Chambers,' of course."

Chapter 41

Photos and Feelings

I WAS SICK OF EVERYTHING. Sick of hiding out and being miserable and alone. Sick of being mad at Mitch and disappointed in my father. All of it. And I was starting to feel constrained in my mom's house. I wanted to be surrounded by my own stuff. I wanted to trip over a gargantuan futon in my tiny living room and cuddle my roommate at night, the big lug.

Lily told me, after about a week of my exile, that Max and his brothers were staging another workday at their mom's house. They had big hopes of finding out more about the mysterious Colin, so I figured that was a perfect time to go get a Lily fix. Seeing my girl always helped me feel better.

We greeted each other like we'd been separated for years, then we flopped onto the couch to catch up. I told her for the first time about my ideas about seeking my master's degree, and she was thrilled for me. Getting her support—and confirmation that maybe it wasn't such a crazy idea for me to become a therapist— felt great. So great, in fact, that I then felt brave enough to open up about Mitch.

"Lils, I did something stupid," I began. "I sort of fell in love with Mitch."

"Oh, yeah, I know," she said, shocking me with her nonchalant reply. "I could see it a million miles away. But why isn't this happy news? I've never seen you fall in love before. Shouldn't we be freaking out and bouncing up and down right now?"

"It might feel like a happier thing if he loved me back," I said, shrugging. "But he doesn't. Not even a little."

"And how do you know that? Did you tell him how you feel?"

"I didn't have to. I made a joke about us going on a date, and he almost swallowed his tongue trying to deny it. It couldn't have been clearer that we weren't on the same page if a skywriter was involved."

"Eh, sometimes it's kind of hard to read those skywriting messages though," she said, looking like she really thought she'd made a decisive point, which made me laugh for the first time in days. That's the thing about Lily—she's the one who always makes everything better, not me, despite what Mitch had tried to assert.

"Yeah, okay, you got me there, I guess."

"Is that the real reason you've been hiding out at your mom's house? You're avoiding him?"

I nodded. "That's a lot of it. Pretty upset about my dad, though, too. That day at Melody's, when Max smiled, I could suddenly see it. I could see my dad's face, and it all kind of came crumbling down on top of me."

"I know it's your father who you're thinking about right now, Claire. But don't shut Max out. He's a mess about all of this, too, and I think it would help both of you to spend some time together. You know, really get to know each other. And maybe, when you're ready, you could tell him about your dad."

"Of course we'll do all those things," I said. "I hope Max doesn't think I'm upset about *him*. Finding out we might be related is the best part of any of this. You and I will really be sisters someday when you two get married."

"Yeah, but you know we're already sisters. I love you, Claire-bear."

"Love you too, Lils," I said. "Always. And, actually, I'm way ahead of you about Max. I used some of my alone time at Mom's this last week to make something for him."

I opened the tote I'd brought along and pulled out the album that I'd made for Max. I spent hours going through a ton of old photos and sneaking shots of them with my phone. I had everything from pictures of Chad and me through the years to a few precious solo shots of my dad and several group pictures of my family. In some of them, I was pretty certain Max would be able to see the similarities to his own reflection that I'd found. I'd even stumbled across a really old album from Dad's childhood, so I threw in some of those younger pictures of him as well. Seeing all this wouldn't be the same for Max as actually getting to meet his father, but maybe it would help.

Lily and I went through the album and talked for hours, and I was shocked to realize it was already late afternoon when we heard Max at the door. I stood up, nervous to see him for some reason, then I got even more nervous when I saw Mitch walk in behind him.

"H-hey," Max said. "C-Claire, it's good to s-see you. We h-have some news, so we w-were going to ask you to c-come over anyway. It's j-just, well, I'm afraid you w-won't like it."

"Oh, uh, okay," I said, tossing a quick wave to my old roommate as though everything was super chill with us. "Hey, Mitch."

The look he gave me in return was loaded with meaning I didn't understand, so I turned my attention back to Max as we all sat down.

"Okay, so what happened?" I asked. "What won't I like?"

"I g-guess we'll never *r-really* know wh-what happened," he started. "But she c-confirmed today that the m-man she keeps c-confusing me with was n-named C-Colin Chambers."

I nodded even as I could feel tears springing to my eyes. What was with me and crying lately?

"I kind of figured that was the case," I finally said. "That night at Melody's…when you smiled? I could see it."

"I'm s-sorry, Claire," he said. "I know this ch-changes your memories of him, which s-sucks."

"It does, and it doesn't," I replied. "Yeah, he apparently cheated on my mom. But you know what? Maybe they separated for a while or something, you know? I don't want to hurt her by asking about it or telling her any of this. But I don't really want to waste energy and years hating him, either. And here's the thing—through some kind of miracle, he just reached out from beyond the grave and put you, this incredibly amazing man, in my life. It's almost like a present from him, even though of course I thought I'd never have any contact from him again. Does that make any sense?"

"It does," Max said as Lily nodded.

"I was mad at him for years for leaving us," I went on. "But now there are all these questions in my mind about his heart attack. Maybe the stress of the secret was killing him. Maybe he tried to fight for you, and that's when your dad found out. When my dad got super stressed, he stuttered. If your dad suspected his wife cheated, and they had a confrontation that brought out my dad's stutter, then he heard you develop a stutter, too…well, maybe that's how he found out. And maybe it was too much for my dad. I guess what I'm trying to say is that I hope it means he fought for you. I *want* it to mean that. Because then his death isn't meaningless anymore."

"I'm p-proud to have you for a s-sister," Max told me then. "Actually, y-you're already the b-best sister I have."

"Oh, I'm something alright," I replied, laughing at his dopey joke and falling back on my own reflexes of jokes-as-armor. "Actually, you're right that I'm awesome, because I brought you something."

I watched as he tentatively turned the pages of the album, closely examining each picture and talking with Lily about the similarities they were noticing. I smiled at the sight, then I lifted my gaze and connected with Mitch's for the first time since he walked in.

"Claire, can we talk?" he asked, causing both Max and Lily to look up at me, too.

"Uh, sure, talk," I said.

"Privately. Please?"

I nodded, rolled my eyes at Lily, and followed him to the door.

I guess we were doing this.

Chapter 42

The Goodbye

HE'D CLEANED. That was the first thing I noticed when we walked into "our" apartment. The place was sparkling. He'd even folded the futon, so it wasn't eating the entire room anymore.

"Wow, you've been busy," I said. "I should go away more often."

"I just wanted to make sure it was presentable," Mitch said. "You know, before I leave."

"Oh, okay, thanks...." Disappointment made the words catch in my throat. "So, what? This is goodbye?"

"Yeah, I'm not sure exactly what my plan is long term, but at the very least I need to get back to work," he said, shoving his hands into the pockets of his jeans. "I thought I'd take on some jobs while I was here, but I never felt up to anything my agent suggested. This whole thing with Max, and your dad, and secrets...I don't know. It's too much."

"Yeah...." Disappointment was still throttling the words I really wanted to say deep inside me. I needed to get over myself quickly, though, because this was my opportunity to try to get him to stay. Part of me desperately wanted to blurt out all my feelings and take that chance. I mean, he was leaving anyway, so what would it hurt? On the other hand, there were things like pride and self-preservation to think about. Indecision left me standing there, mute and uncertain.

"I've missed you," he said, finally breaking the

silence that had descended on us like a dark fog. Things had never been this awkward between us before. Not ever. I hated that this is where we'd ended up.

"You missed me, but not so much that it's stopping you from flying away, though, huh?" I said, a burst of anger yanking my old pal sarcasm right out of me. "Way to overcome, champ."

"Don't," he said, shaking his head and pulling his hands back out of his jeans before tightening them into fists at his side. "Don't do that. Don't crack a bunch of jokes and make it seem like the friendship that grew between us wasn't real or important. I couldn't have done any of this without you, and that's the truth. I don't know how you did it, but you reached deep inside of me and rearranged things for the better. Jake pointed out today that I don't really seem angry anymore, and I kinda think he's right. And I also think it's because of you and your friendship."

"And you did the same things for me," I replied immediately. "Yeah, I still fall back on snark and sarcasm when I don't know how else to handle something. But I'm *trying* to be a better person, and that's because of you. You made me…want more, I guess."

"Me, too," he said, a corner of his mouth lifting into a reasonable impression of a smile. "So, yeah, I'm leaving, but it's also true that a part of me is staying right here, with you."

"But you don't feel more for me, is that right?" I asked, shocked that I actually went there. I suppose it was inevitable, though, since I've never been known for my ability to hold thoughts inside discreetly. "We're friends, but that's it? Just trying to clarify here."

"That's why you pulled away, isn't it?" he asked,

avoiding the actual question. "It wasn't about your dad or Max or any of that. You dropped my friendship and treated me like none of what we had mattered because I was surprised when you casually used the word 'dating' in a sentence? Claire, come on. That's stupid."

"It wasn't my word choice that surprised you," I said, feeling my anger start to simmer now. "And it didn't feel so stupid when the very concept of dating me made you turn green. No, that felt more like embarrassment. Yeah, we were friends. But good old Claire didn't understand all the subtle subtext, just like normal, huh? What is it, my big mouth? Is that what you don't like? Or maybe you're not attracted to me because I'm definitely not as beautiful as you and the whole Tifanee crowd, right? Would I embarrass you at all your sexy model conventions or something?"

"There are no conventions," he said. His exasperation and dorky retort were both things that would have made me laugh under normal circumstances. But this conversation was anything but normal. "You're one of the most beautiful women I've ever seen," he continued, "both in your physical looks and in the incredible strength that emanates from you. Actually, I think pretty much everything about you is amazing. But you didn't talk to me about your feelings, and you sure didn't bother asking me about mine. You just ran off and hid."

"Oh really? That's pretty interesting, considering it's precisely what you're doing right this very minute. But, okay, I'll bite: Tell me about your feelings."

"Fine. A huge part of me wants more, too. I've never wanted it all before—you know, waking up together for the rest of our lives, marriage, kids, and all that. I've never pictured any of that stuff with anyone before you came along. You didn't read anything wrong; of course you didn't. My feelings were right there in every laugh and hug and touch that we shared. But…it's not enough. No, I said that wrong—*I'm* not enough. I don't think I have anything left inside me to give. I'm broken, Claire."

"Right," I said. "Broken. Wow, you really drew the short straw, huh? Because everyone else in this family totally has it all together."

"You're throwing sarcasm at me right now? Seriously? I'm not joking around here. Do you know how isolated and angry and out of touch I've been all these years? Do you know what the day my family fell apart *did* to me? You must have no idea, because if you did, you wouldn't be trying to turn this into one of your jokes."

"*Nothing* about this is funny, Mitch. Even I understand that. But nothing about you is permanently broken. Do you think Max should have stayed locked in silence forever? I mean, gee, he was pretty broken after that day, too, wasn't he? But he's brave and strong. He saw love, and he took a chance. He reached out and grabbed it. And Lily loves him no matter what. Remember? He said her love fills him up and leaves no room for anger. Why can't you try to find the same thing?"

He shook his head. "Max's situation is different. I can't do this. I have to go back and think about everything. I just…I need to go."

"Yeah, sure, okay," I said, my heart shattering inside my chest. Pride made me hope he couldn't see how much he was devastating me. "Think how lucky we both are. We're about to have all the time in the world, all alone forever, just rattling around with no pesky emotional attachments getting in our way. Maybe we'll even forget any of this ever happened. Yay us."

"Can't imagine I could ever forget you," he replied, apparently giving up trying to get me to stop being sarcastic. Smart plan, because it was a losing battle. When I'm upset, I turn into a sarcasm blowtorch. And I was incredibly upset just then.

"Why weren't Melody and Jake's problems too big to overcome, huh?" I asked. "Why weren't Max and Lily's? What makes you so special and super unlovable?"

"Everything," he said, agony creasing his gorgeous face. "You don't see how messed up I am for some reason, but it's all right there. Sure, we could try dating for a while, but I'd destroy it eventually because of my anger and unhappiness and inability to connect. I just would, and I don't want to do that to you. I don't want to do that to *us.*"

"Right," I said again, closing my eyes. I didn't want to look at his pain anymore, not when he was choosing to roll around in despair over a chance at building something potentially fantastic with me. "Giving up without trying is a way better idea. Well, I guess it's time to launch this dumb plan of yours, huh? So...bye, I guess."

"Can I...can I maybe get a goodbye hug?" he asked.

"Sure," I said, stiffly walking into his arms. I tried to capture the moment in my mind so I could hold onto it forever. The feel of his muscled arms around me, the softness of his long hair brushing up against my face, and the familiar spice of his scent all imprinted themselves on my soul. I'd never get over this man.

"Have a nice flight," I told him, pulling back finally, unable to continue torturing myself by lingering in his embrace for too long. I needed to get out of there before I burst into tears or started begging.

"You too," he said, then he rolled his eyes up to the side in a funny, questioning look as he realized what he said.

"Yeah, I'm not flying anywhere, doofus," I replied, pulling the door open before turning around to grab one last look. "For what it's worth, I think you're smart and funny and kind of awesome and, yeah, maybe a little broken, but so what? Newsflash: I'm broken, too. But you know how you wrap your arms around me every night, and that's when you finally find enough peace to sleep? That's just our broken, jagged edges matching up and snapping together perfectly. You've got free will, and I clearly can't stop you. But when you're sitting alone in your apartment in California and unable to sleep, think about that. Maybe you're broken because we're only whole when we're together."

That speech felt a lot like a mic drop, and I was trying to pat myself on the back for how cool it sounded as I stalked away from the apartment.

But as I drove back to my mom's house, all I felt was alone.

Chapter 43

Searching for Answers

MAYBE YOU'RE BROKEN because we're only whole when we're together....

I couldn't get her words out of my head. I mean, yeah, I still did what I said I was going to do—I left town the morning after we said goodbye, returned to my apartment, and threw myself into work. I accepted any stupid gig Janet came up with, and I even flew to a few location shoots. Anything. I was trying to do absolutely anything to get my mind off how much her words were haunting me.

I missed her sass. And her jokes. And her maniacal hoarding of chips. And the loving way she always supported me. And the way she tried to fight for me. And....

Okay, I admit I wasn't doing such a great job of getting my mind off her.

She was right there in every thought I had, like my own personal ghost. Part of me really did want to exorcise her from my head, but my heart wasn't having any of it.

Claire wasn't all I missed though. I missed my brothers, too. I missed the sense of family, and I couldn't believe I'd lasted—alone and on the opposite side of the country—as long as I had.

So all of that missing I was doing was forcing me to re-examine my list of reasons I'd used to convince myself to leave. I'd told Claire I was too broken, and then she'd made that statement that continued scrolling through my mind like a stock ticker—

Maybe you're broken because we're only whole when we're together.

Those words haunted me to the point that I started to believe I must have messed up big time in leaving. I mean, really, what should broken people do if they want to be whole again? Reach out to other people for help was the obvious answer, but of course that's not what I'd done at all. Hiding in isolation was all I knew, after all. That's what I'd been *programmed* to do. And now I felt guilty for it. For everything, really. I felt guilty for leaving both times—years ago and then just recently. I felt guilty for holding on to so many secrets for so long. But I felt guilty about returning and letting all those secrets out, too. After all, Claire never would have discovered that her dad had an affair if it hadn't been for me. I had oceans of remorse inside me because I knew I'd hurt her in my struggle to free myself.

But...I *was* free from the secrets now. And, yes, they'd definitely caused a lot of pain. But they'd had some good effects too, right? Jake and Max had been successful in getting Mom to the doctor, and hopefully the doctor would be able to stem her dementia or whatever. I don't think we would have caught it as quickly if seeing Max hadn't thrown her into the past the way it had. So discovering she needed help was a good result. And Max was truly happy to learn my dad wasn't his, something no one could blame him for. Plus, Claire was relieved to understand a bit more about her father and his death at such a young age. That had been a good thing in its own way, too.

So I guess I could make an argument that my secrets had ended up doing some good after all. And releasing them should have set me free, too. So why didn't I feel free? Why, when Claire was asking me to stay and claim the relationship that was already growing between us, did I choose exile and isolation again? Nothing was forcing me to be alone anymore. I chose that. But why?

These thoughts rolled through me for days. Unfortunately, I found myself unable to find any answers to the questions in my head: I thought of myself as too broken, but why? What was holding me captive in that misery?

When I'd finally had enough of the confusion and pain, I picked up the phone and called Jake. I still didn't have any answers, but I did know I couldn't do it all alone anymore.

"Hey, good to hear from you, bro," he said. "We miss you."

"Miss you guys, too," I said, emotions rising and making those words crackle in my throat.

"Made any decisions?" he asked. "Got a long-term plan yet? You've got to know we're all praying that you get your butt back here."

"I want that, too. But I feel trapped here, like I want to leave but can't. I told Claire I'm too broken to be with her, but I think I got it backward. I think I'm too broken to be without her. But something's stopping me, and I don't know what it is."

"Hmm...have you truly tried to figure it out? Gotten yourself a therapist, maybe? I know you encouraged Claire to start down that career path—she started online classes, by the way—so you must believe that therapy is a real thing that helps people. Did you get that help for yourself?"

"No," I said, feeling foolish. Honestly, I'd never

seriously considered looking for a therapist. But after everything our family had been through, we should probably shop around for some sort of volume discount.

"Listen, I don't have all the answers," Jake continued. "You're going to have to figure this out yourself. But my guess is that your decision-making skills and ability to make plans for your future got stunted by Dad. He forced this role on you, this 'guardian of the truth' thing you've been carrying for so long. But guess what? He's dead. The secrets are out. So you don't have to man your post anymore."

"Yeah, maybe that's what it is," I said, sorting and analyzing his words in my mind. I mean, none of it was a huge revelation, and some version of it had occurred to me already. But maybe not the part about me not having any practice making decisions for my own life.

"From the outside, this all seems kind of easy to me," he went on. "Pack up your crap, load it onto a truck, and get yourself out here. And then find a therapist. I started seeing one after my health scare so I could learn better stress management, and I'd definitely recommend him to you. But it doesn't matter who you see as long as you're trying to get help. And then I think you should show up on the door of a certain neighbor of Max's who seems to be missing you like crazy."

"I miss her, too," I said, realizing that I had started smiling at the mention of her. "A lot."

"I doubt she expects you to be perfect, Mitch. All of us are works in progress. She told Max she's been trying to work on that sarcastic side of hers, but I don't know how well that's going. She's had her joke-o-meter set on 'stun' since you left."

"I'll bet," I said, chuckling now.

"Mitch, having you leave was Dad's plan, not yours. Don't let him make any other decisions for you, okay? He didn't do such a great job making decisions for himself, after all. This is the guy you want running your life?"

He was right—being back in California was Dad's plan for my life, not mine. That's what was broken inside me. I'd become the man my dad wanted me to be, and it was time to change that. I wasn't going to let him win. Enough was enough.

As soon as the call with Jake was over, I went online to check out moving companies.

Chapter 44

Nothing Left Unsaid

WHEN MITCH LEFT, I grieved the loss like it was a death. I mean, it *was* the death of my dreams for what we could have had together. My love for him didn't seem to be going away, though. Somehow it was defying all logic and expanding inside me instead. Also, it wasn't exactly easy to forget him when I was around his twin brother all the time. Seeing Mitch's face on Jake was definitely adding to my pain.

But I allowed myself to go through the stages of grief, starting—of course—with denial. I was absolutely convinced he'd come running back to me full of apologies for leaving in the first place.

When that didn't happen, I spent days being mad at him. That ridiculously beautiful man with his annoying collection of problems he couldn't work through.

When *that* stage was over, I had to process a lot of self-doubt and remorse. Maybe it was all my fault. Maybe because I'm such a tactless mess, my love wasn't big enough or good enough to help him overcome his demons.

I was stranded somewhere in the middle of the whole self-doubt thing when Lily intervened.

"Nope," she said when I opened the door, her knock summoning me out of a tortilla-chip-fueled pity party. "This isn't happening."

"Oh, sure it is," I replied, standing back to let her

in. "But just so we're both on the same page here, what are you talking about?"

"This whole Mitch-depression thing you're in." She grabbed my hand and led me to the futon. "Talk to me."

I slumped onto the futon in defeat. "He left. I wasn't enough. Being with me wasn't enough. My *love* wasn't enough."

"Uh-huh, okay. Just so I understand all of this, you actually said those words to him? You stood right in front of him and said, 'Mitch, you gorgeous hunk of a man, I love you'?"

"No, not exactly. But it was implied. I said I had feelings for him. I think I did, anyway. We definitely talked about being together and stuff. But he said if we tried to date, his anger would eventually ruin everything."

"Wait, you let him leave without fully throwing your heart on the floor and articulating precisely how you feel?" There was incredulity all over her face now. "My strong, incredibly brave Claire, who says any crazy thought that occurs to her in any situation? *You* left something as important as love unsaid?"

My teeth were clenched together now. "Umm… yes?"

"Who even *are* you?" she said, her nose crinkling as she studied me. "When I realized I had feelings for Max and I thought he lived in California, I bought myself a ticket and marched straight to his door to claim my man. You're not willing to do the same thing? So again, who are you? And seriously, what have you done with my Claire?"

She was so right. I *hadn't* come out and clearly told him I loved him. If I was going to lose this fight, it wasn't going to be because I hadn't said everything on my mind and in my heart. Not me, the person who normally wasn't afraid to say anything regardless of the consequences.

So, now that I had a plan, I got his address from Lily and bought a ticket to California.

*   *   *

When he opened the door to his apartment, the shock was very clear on his face.

He stepped back wordlessly and gestured for me to walk inside. I wasn't prepared for exactly how happy I'd feel to see him again. And I wasn't prepared for what I saw once I was in there, either—stacks and stacks of moving boxes were piled everywhere I could see.

"Wow," I said. "I've never seen such a well-executed example of early American moving-box design and decor."

"I'm glad you like what I've done with the place," he replied, a lazy smile on his face now.

"I really do." I wanted to read all kinds of things into what I was seeing, but I tried to dial back my expectations. He could be moving to Tibet, for all I knew. "What does this mean, Mitch?"

"I think you know. What does you standing here in front of me with a rolling suitcase mean?"

"I think you probably know that, too. But you know me, talking's my specialty, so I guess I'll spell it out for you."

"I'd expect nothing else. Claire's gonna Claire."

"Yes, exactly. You get me."

"I can't tell you how much I've missed this," he said with that chuckle I'd been dying to hear again. "How much I've missed *you.*"

I couldn't help smiling. "I missed you, too. I spent

some time being mad at you for rejecting what I was offering and leaving town. But Lily pointed out that I never really told you everything. I mean, I hinted I had feelings and wanted more than friendship, but I didn't come out and say it."

"Say what?" he asked, his voice a throaty whisper.

"That I love you," I said. "I never actually said those words, but they're true. I love your sense of humor, and how it's got a sharper edge to it than either of your brothers'. I love laughing with you or just chilling and doing nothing on the futon. I love how much family means to you, and I love that you were willing to toss your whole life away simply to protect them. I love that you understand me and accept me for who I am, and I love that you pull all the good stuff out of me while accepting the bad. And of course I love that you're this physically perfect eye candy, but I'd be lying if I didn't admit that I stopped thinking about you that way. I no longer see the model because I now see the man underneath. *He's* the guy I love, and he's the guy I don't want to live without. I tried it, and it sucks. If you want me to move with you to Tibet, then I'll do it. Just let me love you, and everything else will work out."

"Tibet?" he asked, his eyebrows furrowing into a cute bit of confusion.

"That was your takeaway from all of that?"

Now he was smiling, too. "I'm not moving to Tibet, Claire. But if I were, I'd definitely want you to come along. I tried being without you, too, and I agree that it sucks. I can't stop thinking about you. I can't sleep. I can't eat. And you were right when you said without you I'm not whole. So what I'm trying to say here is that I love you, too. I love your sass and your sarcasm and your jokes, and I love that you're brave enough to let them fly no matter what. I love that you're taking on this new challenge of pursuing your career, and that you're not letting fears or doubts stop you. I love that you accepted Max into your heart immediately and never made him feel like any of what happened was his fault. I love how ferociously you love and support Lily. And I love that, in your arms, I find the only true peace I've ever known."

"Okay, good. So then, yeah...what's with the boxes?" I asked, a dopey look on my face now that didn't fully reflect the full-on happiness fireworks display erupting inside me then.

"If you hadn't initiated this conversation we're having here, I was going to show up at your door and do it there," he replied. "There's no world where you and I can be apart. It's just not a thing."

"I agree. And I even brought you something to show you how serious I am about this."

"You brought me something?"

"Yeah, hang on." I slid my backpack off and rooted around inside before finding and pulling out his gift. "Here, this is for you."

"You bought me Doritos?" he asked, a huge smile I'd never before seen on his face revealing about twenty teeth in its wide expanse. "Cool ranch? Party size? Wow—you really *are* serious, aren't you?"

"I am," I said, handing it to him and laughing as he pretended to inspect his gift from all sides like a rare jewel.

"Would you be offended if I said there's something else I'd rather have right now?"

"More than Doritos?" I asked. "I mean, I might be a *little* offended, yeah. But what is it?"

"You," he said, tossing the bag on the nearest stack of boxes and opening his arms to me. I launched myself at him and not-so-delicately whumped right into his chest.

He wasted no time pulling me into one of those swoony kisses you normally only see in movies, and I found myself threading my fingers into his hair and feeling the scratch of his sexy scruff on my face as we explored each other with a fevered chemistry like I'd never experienced before. He made me feel beautiful and loved and treasured all at once, and it felt like I could be happy kissing him for the rest of my life and never tire of it. From the look on his face when we finally pulled apart, he'd felt some of those fireworks exploding in his chest, too.

"Yeah," I said, breathless now. "Your idea was way better than Doritos."

"Strong words," he said. "And so you know, I can't ever remember being this happy before. Thanks for being who you are, Claire. Thank you for loving me enough to fight for me."

"Always," I said. And I meant it, too. After all, honesty's my thing, right? I never say stuff I don't mean. I'd told Mitch I loved him, and I meant those words with everything inside me. He was never going to be lonely again.

I'd make sure of it.

Chapter 45

Good News

"WE'VE GOT good news," Melody said, finally sitting down and joining us at the table in their new house. She'd been fussing in the kitchen over the meal for way too long while refusing offers of help, so it was good to see her finally relax for a minute. "Liam? Do you want to tell them?"

"Yeah," Liam said, looking proud and important in his role as news giver. "I'm gonna be a big brother, just like my dad is."

The reaction of everyone at the table was an initial shocked silence, followed by a whole lot of happy gasping.

"Yeah," Jake said, with a laugh as he ruffled Liam's hair. "First off, Melody's pregnant. And second, this guy asked if he could start calling me dad now."

"P-pretty smart," Max said nodding his head at Liam. "You c-can't find a better d-dad than J-Jake."

"I ran it by Ron and Celeste first," Melody said. "I know that as Dan's parents, they're going to find that a little painful to hear. But they support us and love us, and in the end, they were fine with it. Actually, they asked if they could be grandparents to the new baby, too, and of course we said yes."

"I'm excited about being a grandmother to both Liam and his new sibling, too," my mom said, and Melody reached over to squeeze her hand. A new medication had given her a lot more lucidity, and we were able to coax her out of her house a bit more lately.

"So happy for you, brother," I said, looking at Jake now. "Max is right. Liam and this new baby are the luckiest kids in the world."

The conversation moved from there to things like due dates and baby showers and baby names. To be honest, I got a little lost in all of it. I was too busy gazing at the beautiful woman by my side. Since the day she showed up in California to itemize all her feelings for me, my life had turned around. The angry loner who didn't understand precisely what was broken inside him was long gone. In his place was the new man I was only becoming because I was standing in the sunlight of Claire's love. It's not like I could have pushed her away from me for long anyway, though, because Jake had been right about her. She was feisty. She could totally take down a grizzly if she felt like it. She sure helped me defeat my inner demons.

I tuned back to the happy chatter when Lily's voice emerged above it all.

"We kind of have a couple things to be happy about, too," she said, flashing a smile meant only for Max before turning back to meet our expectant gazes. "Not as wonderful as a baby for sure, but we're excited that we decided to save up to buy a house."

"I'm s-sick of that apartment," Max added. "I was s-stuck there way too long. But my b-business is growing, and Lily n-needs a place to write, too. We need something b-big enough to offer office s-space to both of us, b-basically."

"And that's the other bit of news," Lily said, picking up the conversation where Max dropped it, as though they'd rehearsed ahead of time. "I finally finished my first book. Well, I have a rough draft anyway."

Claire emitted a sound that could only be described as a squeal, and everyone offered their more toned-down congratulations, too.

I realized then that our family really was changing and growing—and all of it for the better. With the chains of our past finally broken, it seemed like the possibilities were suddenly endless for the Cruz and Chambers clan.

"Listen, I can't let all of this happy news happen without adding something of our own," I said, reaching under the table for Claire's hand. She squeezed mine in reply and then leaned over to plant a quick kiss on my cheek.

"Oh no," Jake said, mock horror on his face. "Not another one of Mitch's secrets."

"S-seriously," Max added. "It's g-gotten to the point that I d-don't even want to s-sit at a table with you anymore."

"Look, honey," Claire said. "I'm not the only one popping out jokes in this family."

"Oh no, I think we're in for it," I said, rolling right along with her. "Those genes ran strong in you and Max, at least. Okay, well, I guess you guys don't want to know my latest secret, so move on. Anyone have anything else to share?"

"Oh no you don't!" Melody protested. "It's our table, and Jake and I demand you spill it! What's your news?"

"I swear I'm not about to lob one of my old secret grenades at you guys again," I assured them with a chuckle as I lifted Claire's hand so everyone could see it clearly. "This time it's a good thing—I asked this beautiful lady to marry me, and she said yes."

There were more gasps and congratulations and

excited discussions about things like wedding dates and locations. I let Claire answer all the questions—who better than her to lay out the truth, after all?

As for me, I just sat back and surveyed our family. I met Jake's gaze, and he nodded. Call it the twin connection, but I knew precisely what we both were thinking: Our family had been through the fire over the years. Pain and loss and heartache had devastated each of us in one way or another during that time. But we'd reached the other side and found love, peace, and joy along the way. We'd conquered our demons and all the hateful secrets that had separated and defeated us for so long. And I think that was the main takeaway in all of it: When we were apart, we were weaker. But together? Together we were unstoppable.

I leaned over and planted a lingering kiss on my fiancée.

"What was that for?" she asked, offering me the wide smile that had become her default expression.

"Just because I love you," I said. Actually, I loved every single person at that table. Max had been right. Love really does fill you up and push out all the hate.

Clinking glasses and chattering voices filled the room as we all enjoyed our meal and discussed our future plans, and a feeling of peace seemed to settle over all of us. After all, that dinner marked the first day of all our bright and happy tomorrows.

Thank You!

Thank you for reading Mitch and Claire's story! I would appreciate it so much if you took a moment to rate or review it on your favorite site.

There's more Mitch and Claire—as well as the entire Cruz family—in books one and two of the series. If you read this book first, be sure to loop back and see how it all started with one huge crush on a certain bubbly neighbor....

Stay to the end for a look at Max's story, *The Distance Between Us: A Hidden-Identity Romance*. Max has been locked in silence and trauma for years. But his crush on his sweet and bubbly neighbor Lily has him searching for the doors of his prison.

But first up is a sneak peek of my next release, *Thrown: A Baseball Romance*, which is book three in The Curveball Incident Series. Zeke was on the brink of an exciting new opportunity when his brother Zach's life imploded, taking Zeke's dreams out with the shrapnel from the choices he made. Zach might have gotten his life back on track, but Zeke's been stuck ever since in a life he never planned for and sure didn't want. Can he move past his resentments and capture his old dream of working for the Yankees, or are some dreams too far out of reach? And what should he do about his growing feelings of attraction for a younger woman he has no business letting into his heart?

THROWN: A BASEBALL ROMANCE

Prologue

"THE *YANKEES?!*" Zeke asked, his eyes popping open wide and his mouth hanging slack as he waited for confirmation and worked to process what he'd just heard. Despite how short that two-word punch of information was, soaking in the meaning it held was no simple task. Hearing there might be a scout from the Yankees in the crowd was the easy part; grasping the enormity of that message was a much, *much* steeper hill to climb. "No, wait, you're messing with me right now. Knock it off."

"Zeke, man, I'm serious!" Freddy said, none of his usual playfulness evident on his face now. "My dad heard Coach Mac talking to someone in the stands."

"Who?" Zeke asked, impatience flooding him now. He was ready to grab his teammate and rattle the information out of him if necessary. "Who was Coach talking to?"

"I don't know," he said, shrugging and lifting his arms up in the universal sign of confusion and lack of information. "Do you want to hear what I *do* know, or do you want to keep interrupting me?"

"Would you just come on and tell me?" Zeke said, trying to chill out…but failing miserably. His heart was thumping such a driving beat that it seemed like Freddy should be able to hear it booming in his chest.

"Okay, so like I said, Coach was talking to some guy, and my dad heard him say something about a friend of a friend who knows a Yankee scout," Freddy said, the words tumbling out of him now. "And the friend of the friend of Coach's told him about you, and the scout came tonight to check you out!"

"Me?!" Zeke said, not sure at all that he followed any of that friend-of-a-friend craziness, but he wasn't dumb enough to miss the basic meaning: This might just be the most important opportunity of his entire life. Sure, he was only seventeen, but if he could pitch a lights-out game and catch the interest of this scout, his dreams could one day come true. Not only could he start down a path that might lead to the pitching mound in a Major League game, but it could be the pitching mound at Yankee Stadium. That was it. *That* was Zeke's dream.

Sure, he grew up in Texas, so his dream didn't make a whole lot of sense, maybe, at least from the outside. But that's what he'd always, *always* wanted to do: pitch for the Yankees. Whitey Ford, Ron Guidry, Don Larsen and his perfect game in the World Series, Mariano Rivera…there had been so many legendary pitchers for the team, and he knew the stats for all of them. Heck, Babe Ruth had even pitched a few games for the Yankees. But since two players who went to high school in Texas, Roger Clemens and Andy Pettitte, made it big on the team, that solidified the goal in Zeke's mind. One day the name Hiller would join that line-up of pitching stars; he knew it as surely as he knew his own name. And that was *before* he found out that his coach's friend's friend's…whatever actually knew a team scout.

It seemed too perfect. Like destiny had shown up at his front door and reached out to ring the bell. As well as he knew anything in his life, he knew he'd be opening that door wide with a huge sloppy grin on his face.

"No pressure, boys," Coach Mac said, suddenly appearing from who knows where. "But I need some big focus and even bigger hustle out there tonight. We've got some visitors in the stands who we want to impress. Zeke, you need to go through your warm-ups and then go through them again. I need you nice and limber and ready to throw fire tonight, you got me?"

"Yeah Coach, I got you," Zeke said, excitement fluttering in his chest now. Coach had all but confirmed what Freddy's dad overheard. There *was* someone special in those stands tonight, and that someone might hold in their hands the ability to help him make his crazy pinstriped dreams come true.

This was really it. One day he'd be able to look

back at this moment and know it was the start of absolutely everything for him. The vision he had in his head, the one where he was standing on the mound under the bright lights of Yankee Stadium, fueled him as he got dressed and then cycled through his stretches. It burned in his chest as he threw his warm-up pitches. It stamped itself on his soul when he took a no-hitter into the fourth inning.

And in the fifth inning, when searing pain ripped through his shoulder and down his arm, causing him to scream in agony and fall to his knees on the mound, it flickered and died.

THE DISTANCE BETWEEN US: A HIDDEN-IDENTITY ROMANCE

Max's Story

Chapter 1

I NOTICED the exact moment it happened, the agonizing instant the light in her face disappeared behind dark clouds of sadness.

I knew precisely when it happened because I'm observant like that. Plus...well, okay, it was mostly because I've been lurking around and crushing on Lily like a starstruck fanboy ever since she moved into the apartment next to mine almost a year ago. I know all her usual expressions now. Although, to be totally honest, her typical look is whatever expression says "bubbly." Like she was created in a cheerfulness lab and came preset with all the default factory settings. She's...okay, I know this is super corny, but she's *sunshine.* Her rays pull me in like nothing I've ever experienced before, because if she's sunshine...I don't know...but I think maybe I'm an eclipse.

It happened immediately for me, that sizzle of awareness and attraction, and I hadn't even seen her gorgeous face yet. I was instantly on high alert from the day she moved in just from the sound of her sweet voice. I was home working—because I don't really go anywhere else—when I heard the banging noises and the grunts and strains of her friends and family as they lifted her furniture and thumped her boxes and knickknacks into those small rooms. The walls are thin enough that I knew right away the new tenant had arrived. But that wasn't what caught my attention. After all, I hadn't exactly been enthralled by the previous one, whose name may or may not have been Gus. The most interaction we ever had was me sometimes cautiously waving hello and him reluctantly nodding back.

But Lily's moving day? *That* I noticed. Her infectious happiness can seep right through the walls, apparently, because I heard the silver peals of her laughter and the musical lilt of her chatter, and that was it. I was hooked. Because of *course* she could make even moving into a dumpy apartment sound like eating an ice cream cone on a summer day at a carnival. And, honestly, from that day on, I've been utterly jealous of anyone lucky enough to be on the other side of that wall—and on the receiving end of one of those precious smiles.

Even if we weren't neighbors, I still would have noticed her. She's so consistently *up*, no matter what boring stuff she's doing. Checking the mail? She'll laugh and chat with anyone who happens to be in the lobby. Separating her whites and colors in the laundry room?

She's joking with the janitor, who knows her by name—because of course he does—or any of the other tenants who happen to be nearby. She's optimistic, radiant, and outgoing—basically everything I'm not. I guess that's why I can't get her out of my head. Opposites attracting and all that. I'm the weary wanderer dying of thirst in the desert, and Lily is the crystal glass of refreshing, ice-cold water. And that potentially lifesaving drink is, ultimately, out of my reach.

That's the problem right there. Despite being my neighbor, Lily isn't within my reach. No, not me. Not good old, socially shutdown Max. I'm basically locked in a jail of shyness and anxiety, and I have been since…well, always. But especially since high school. Those years, for me, were like trying to walk into the ocean. You want nothing more than to get your feet under you and find your balance, but meanwhile waves of fear and condemnation are constantly trying to pull you down and sweep you away.

It wasn't even a typical high school thing like you see in the movies. I wasn't unlucky enough to get labeled or lumped in with a group of dorks. I wasn't a band geek or a nerd or a burnout or a gearhead. I was just so lost inside myself that I'm pretty sure no one even knew I'd been there at all. I was like furniture or wallpaper; part of the setting where the action of everyone else's lives took place. I barely registered on any of my classmates'—or teachers'—minds. They didn't talk to me, and I definitely didn't talk to them. I mean, don't get me wrong: I'm glad I don't have a sadsack backstory of being shoved into lockers or wedgied in the middle of the basketball court during homecoming. But to not even be *noticed?* That's a different kind of suffering altogether. So, yeah, I didn't make any waves, but I definitely didn't make any friends, either. I'll bet if you pointed to my picture in the yearbook, most of my former classmates would wonder if I had been included as some kind of a printing error.

After I graduated, as much as I wanted my college degree, I just couldn't force myself to navigate campus life. Dorms? Student organizations and activities? I had managed to bellycrawl through high school, but to keep going in that environment? I just…I couldn't do it. Almost no one in my family was surprised, and I guess they didn't think I could do it, either, because I didn't get a whole lot of pushback. One apartment and one online degree later, and, well…let's just say I've never really faced any of my social challenges head on.

You know what the really crazy part is? I could do okay with women now, looks-wise anyway, if I could just move past all the things that paralyze me and make me want to remain invisible. Here's an irony for you: My brother Jake is a personal trainer and a model. Actually, both my brothers are. They're twins. Mitch and Jake are almost completely covered in tattoos. They both have long hair and huge muscles. They're the types of guys you see on the covers of fitness magazines. And they're confident and tough. In other words, they're everything I'm not.

Mitch lives in California, so we're not exactly close. I don't know him very well at all, I guess, and honestly *no one* really knows me. But Jake, he's absolutely the best. He never gives up trying with me. When the rest of the world decided it had better things to do, Jake stepped in as my protector, advocate, and only friend. So he's a great big brother and way more important to me than I could ever be to him. He basically tackled and shoved my scrawny self into the gym after I moved into my apartment following my altogether undistinguished high school career. He thought it would help me find my confidence; you know, like maybe I dropped it behind the racks of free weights or something.

I'd do almost anything for Jake. I may be stunningly awkward, but I know and appreciate that I won the big-brother lottery. So I started dragging myself out to his gym really early in the mornings, before the crowds come, just to make him happy. As much as I was doing it for him and not for myself, I have to admit, as time has gone on, I've managed to undergo a bit of a post-school transformation as a result of Jake's nagging. I've gradually planked and lifted away some of the gangly awkwardness. I filled out and hardened up—not to Mitch or Jake's levels or anything, but I can definitely see the outside, physical changes for the better that have taken place.

Too bad no amount of cardio or free weights could ever cure the rolling, chaotic mess I've got going on inside my head.

Acknowledgments

I'VE NEVER PARTICIPATED in any writing sprints or in the NaNoWriMo program. I've always just worked at my own slow pace, fitting writing time into whatever free moments I can grab in my normally busy life. That was definitely true of books one and two of this series. I took months to craft each of them, and for some reason I especially had trouble getting Jake's story just right. I'd hit periods of writer's block and have to walk away and try again later.

That is *not* what happened with Mitch and Claire's story! This story seemed to fall out of me faster than I could type the words. It was haunting both my waking hours and at night—I found myself dreaming about it, and I'd have to just get up and start writing again. It was the craziest, most intense writing sprint of my life. In the end, I completed the first draft inside of three weeks!

I'm not sure exactly how this writing sprint came about, but I had a lot of time to devote to it last summer, so that was certainly part of it. And I had a clear vision of what the conflict was for each of these characters, as well as how I wanted the overarching story to wrap up for the entire family. So that clear picture helped me too. But honestly, I think what turbo blasted the story out of me was how fun it was to write the banter and sass of these two characters, especially for Claire. I have always loved snarky characters, and I guess Claire's lack of a filter was the jet fuel I needed.

I hope you enjoyed Mitch and Claire's story, and I'd love to hear your thoughts about it in reviews, on social media, or via email!

As always, I'm sending out all my love and thanks to my family and friends for all their support. And a huge thank you to my friend and editor Wil Mara, who helps me out even in the middle of his own mega-busy life. Thank you!

About the Author

ANNE TROWBRIDGE loves writing romances that hit major emotional beats in swoony, angsty stories in which the couples really earn their happily ever afters. Expect banter, angst, and deeply emotional connections that resonate!

She lives in New Jersey with her husband, two kids, and two dogs. When she's not reading or writing, she's teaching language arts to middle schoolers, which really should involve medals for bravery. She grew up all over the Midwest and somehow still loves to travel and see new places.

Join her and learn more about upcoming books at:

https://www.annetrowbridgebooks.com/

https://linktr.ee/annetrowbridgebooks